MAN OF HIS DREAMS

A HOT NIGHTS IN THE BIG EASY NOVELLA

KIM FIELDING

Tin Box
— PRESS —

CHAPTER

ONE

"But according to my AirTag, my suitcase flew from Oakland and is now stuck in Chicago." Flip Devin tried his best to sound calm and reasonable, even though he felt anything but.

In contrast, the agent on the other end of the line simply sounded bored. "Sir, as I explained, we haven't yet found your luggage piece in the system. We'll notify you when we do."

"I've found it. It's at O'Hare. I, however, am in New Orleans."

"I understand that you're in New Orleans, sir. We're currently attempting to track your luggage piece. You can contact us in the morning for a status update."

Working customer service for an airline was most likely no one's dream job, and this poor guy probably had to deal with a lot of angry and frustrated people on a daily basis. That wouldn't be much fun unless you were a masochist. So Flip was trying really, really hard not to be an asshole. But it wasn't easy.

"Can't you put out some kind of alert for them so they'll search for my bag in Chicago? I can even pinpoint which part of the building it's in."

"Sir, we're currently attempting to track your luggage piece. You can contact—"

"Never mind."

Flip ended the call abruptly—which ordinarily would have made him feel guilty—but it was better than swearing at the agent. Assuming that had actually been an agent on the other end and not a robot. If it was a robot, Flip didn't feel guilty at all.

He set his phone on the couch cushion beside him and glared.

The wayward suitcase wasn't a complete disaster. This apartment had come fully furnished, he'd packed his laptop and a few essentials in his carry-on, and he could venture out tomorrow to buy anything he urgently needed. But he was still annoyed and... uncomfortable. This whole situation was stressful anyway, and he wished he had his favorite old jeans and the ratty Ramones T-shirt he'd been hanging on to since college.

Well, dwelling on the situation wouldn't solve anything. It was nearly midnight, and he'd eaten nothing today except an airport sandwich and a packet of pretzels. After a decent sleep and a good meal in the morning, he'd feel much better, even if his suitcase was still in another state.

With a theatrical groan, he hauled himself off the couch, but instead of heading straight to the bedroom, he decided to give himself a tour of his new home. He'd done a quick walk-through when he first arrived, but he'd been too distracted to pay close attention. Now he could get a better idea of what he was in for, plus he could start a shopping list for the next day. He'd have to find out where the nearest supermarket was and the nearest Target. Hopefully, at least one of them was within walking distance. Living without a car was going to take some getting used to.

The living room wasn't huge, but it had twelve-foot ceilings with decorative cornices. Three French doors—which during the daytime would undoubtedly flood the space with light—led to a balcony overlooking St. Philip Street. The wooden floor looked recently refinished, one wall was exposed brick, and there was a fancy glass chandelier and a nonfunctional fireplace. The couch was comfortable. An antique desk was tucked into one corner. He might want to reorient it to face outside, but that could wait.

The small kitchen was big enough for his needs since he wasn't much of a cook. As far as he could tell, the appliances were pretty new. A little round table with two chairs sat against a wall. Not the most inviting space, but he doubted he'd spend much time there.

Beyond the kitchen was a short hallway that provided access to the bathroom and a couple of closets, and past that lay the bedroom, where the floor plan was nearly identical to the living room. He hoped the morning sun wouldn't shine through the transoms over the draped French doors.

Most of the furnishings were more utilitarian than stylish and the wall art was NOLA-themed but generic. It was fine. He'd be here only three months anyway, which would give him time to decide where he wanted to land more permanently.

Now if only he had his goddamn suitcase.

With that sour thought, he stripped off his clothes and got ready for bed.

The bed and the living room desk were the only pieces of furniture with panache, but whereas the desk was diminutive and delicate, the bed was enormous— a veritable continent with a headboard and footboard ornately carved with stylized vines, flowers, and birds. The motif continued even on the side rails. It looked like something French royalty might have slept in before the Revolution took its grisly turn. The snowy linens felt expensive, and there were a half-dozen pillows. Although Flip was tall, he almost needed a step stool to climb onto the thing. The mattress was exactly firm enough. He might not have his luggage, but he had a magnificent place to sleep.

And that's exactly what he did, almost immediately. None of the restless tossing and turning he'd become accustomed to; he simply laid his head down and immediately fell into a warm, fluffy cloud of nothingness....

And directly into a dream.

He was still in New Orleans, but his new living space was much larger than in reality, with endless rooms branching in every direction. He was searching for his suitcase, which he knew was there. Somewhere. He opened closets and cupboards and door after door, and although he found lots of interesting furniture and knickknacks and several rooms stuffed with books, nothing in this place was his.

The more he looked, the more distressed he became, until finally he found an open French door and stepped outside. "My suitcase is in Chicago, not on a balcony," he said out loud.

"That's a *gallery* you're standing on."

Flip swung around to discover a smiling man standing a few feet away.

It was dark out, and since the balcony—the *gallery* —was poorly lit and the street below contained only a few flickering gas lamps, it was difficult to discern the man's features. He was shorter than Flip by a few inches and wore an old-fashioned suit, complete with tie and pocket square. A Homburg perched on his head at a jaunty angle. All Flip could see of his face was the wide smile.

"A gallery is a place where people hang art," said Flip, obscurely happy to have the chance to argue with someone in his sleep.

"And if a walkway has support poles underneath, it's a gallery. Sometimes words can have more than one meaning, can't they? Like *dream*, for instance. That can signify all sorts of things." The smile increased a notch or two, as if this man also enjoyed a good squabble over something insignificant.

"Fine. Whatever you want to call it, my suitcase isn't here."

"Maybe you're better off without the baggage." The man had an accent. At first Flip thought it was New York, before he realized that it was, of course, New Orleans.

Flip rolled his eyes at the man's comment. "I don't want my subconscious making a whole metaphorical thing over this. I'm missing my real, physical suitcase, which contains most of my earthly possessions and is sitting in O'Hare."

The man came a step closer. "I'm not your subconscious."

"Yeah?" Now Flip crossed his arms.

He could smell the man's cologne—something with spicy, woodsy notes—and somewhere nearby a car stereo banged out a song with a lot of bass. The gallery floor felt a little gritty under his bare feet; the humid air hugged his bare skin. He couldn't recall ever having a dream with such complex sensory information. And although he'd had lucid dreams before, he'd always awakened as soon as he realized what was going on. Not this time.

"What's your name?" the man asked as he moved closer.

"Flip."

That brought a laugh. "What?"

"It's short for Phillip. A stupid childhood nickname

that stuck, and since I'm not too fond of either Phillip or Phil, I haven't tried to shake it." It was also the name that appeared on his book covers.

"Good to meet you, Flip. They used to call me Scratch. 'Cause I know how to cure an itch."

The smile turned into a leer, and Flip was so bemused by the whole situation that he accepted the proffered handshake. Scratch had long, slender fingers with a strong grip.

"Flip and Scratch," Flip muttered. "Sounds like cartoon characters or a really bad board game."

"Where you from, Flip?"

"California."

"Always wanted to go there. Never made it."

Flip felt a little sorry for him, which was ridiculous. "You can go anytime."

"Nah. Too late. I ain't goin' nowhere."

Scratch now stood so close that Flip could finally make out his features. He had an elegant beauty, like a boy-band heartthrob aged gracefully into his early thirties. Delicate arched eyebrows, a strong nose, the kind of mouth that romantic poets liked to describe. Dark eyes, unfathomably deep, which might have been terrifying if not for his easy grin.

"What you doin' here in my city, kid?" Scratch's accent had thickened.

Flip decided he might as well be honest in his sleep. "Withdrawing."

"From what?"

"Bad decisions."

Scratch's low laughter sent a frisson down Flip's spine. "This here ain't no good place for hiding from bad decisions. It's a place for making 'em—and not regretting 'em either." He reached up and ran his thumb across the stubble on Flip's jawline.

And Flip woke up, finding himself in that enormous bed, lost between time zones, and with his cock achingly hard.

CHAPTER

TWO

The suitcase remained in Chicago.

Flip should have gone shopping for essentials as soon as he was up and moving in the morning, but he couldn't get himself into the mood. Instead, after pulling on the fresh set of clothes from his carry-on, he had a pastry and coffee at a charming café on Ursuline Street and then wandered.

Although it was only mid-March, the air was already warm and muggy. He was going to have to get used to the humidity. But unlike his neighborhood back in Oakland, this city was pancake-flat, which made walking easy despite the hazardous sidewalks: their pavement cracked, buckled by tree roots, or missing entirely. At first Flip made his way up to Bourbon Street, but he soon tired of the crowds and strolled down to Chartres Street instead. He then headed out of the French Quarter and into neighborhoods that his phone informed him were called

Marigny and Bywater. Fewer tourists here, by far, although the architecture still looked exotic compared to that of the West Coast.

Eventually he found himself in a park along the river, where he stood at a railing and looked out over the muddy water. Big ships passed, tugboats pushed barges, and somewhere someone played a mournful tune on a saxophone. *This could be a scene in a movie*, he thought. *Flip Devin is….* He wasn't sure how to finish that title. What *was* he?

The answer came to him in Scratch's voice: *You're lost, kid.*

Well, maybe. And his phone GPS wasn't going to help this kind of lost. He'd just have to find his way home on his own—wherever that home might end up being.

He passed a small market not too far from his apartment and picked up enough basic food items to fill a couple of plastic shopping bags. He'd gone about a block when his phone buzzed. After a few moments of trying to juggle phone and bags, he set down the groceries so he could check the message. It was from the airline, informing him that his luggage was on its way to New Orleans. Which initially heartened him, until he followed up by tracking the AirTag and discovered that now his suitcase was back in Oakland, where it had started.

Lovely. He sat on a bench in the shade and made another call to customer service. The rep insisted that his luggage piece would arrive any time now.

All the way home and then while he put his purchases away, he reminded himself that he wouldn't die without the contents of that suitcase. Nothing in there was irreplaceable. He'd never owned much that had sentimental value, and the items he did possess—along with his embarrassingly large book collection—were currently tucked away in a storage unit in Berkeley. He couldn't really explain why his wayward stuff was causing him so much distress, but his jaw was clenched and his shoulders were tight.

One of the hallway closets contained a small washer/dryer unit. He put in all of yesterday's clothes and then spent a chunk of time figuring out how to get the thing started. It was a waste to run such a small load, but otherwise he'd be out of clean clothes by tomorrow. Unless a miracle happened and his suitcase showed up. He didn't dare hope.

What he needed was to get some work done. That was a good distraction, and his deadlines weren't going to meet themselves.

He maneuvered the little desk—heavier than it looked—so that it faced one of the tall windows, then brewed himself a cup of coffee, sat down, and fired up his laptop. Because he couldn't help himself, he checked on the suitcase again and found it still in Oakland, which spurred him to do an online chat with an airline customer service rep who assured him that his luggage piece was on its way to New Orleans. Finally, he opened his current manuscript.

The page just sat there, cursor blinking.

He was thirty-two-thousand words into this novel, which would have been fine if he hadn't also been thirty-two-thousand words into it last week. And the week before that. And, okay, the week before *that*. He wasn't even sure if it was writer's block or simply a crisis of confidence, because during the past month he'd typed thousands of words and then deleted every one of them because they felt stupid. His muse, it seemed, was as lost as he was.

Today he clicked away for an hour or so, until he realized that not only was the entire scene wildly out of character for his protagonist, but Flip had also written himself into a corner and had no idea how to get out. Growling, he highlighted the whole section and made it disappear.

Maybe another walk would help.

This time he stopped for a late lunch at a place on Decatur and wondered how long he could last on a diet of étouffée, jambalaya, gumbo, and red beans and rice. With beignets added for good measure.

Fortified, he set out again and eventually made his way to the Garden District, where he gawked at the mansions and avoided stumbling over the tree roots that breached the sidewalks. Azaleas bloomed behind iron fences, crows called from rooftops, and Mardi Gras beads hung from mossy tree limbs.

He set up camp for a bit in a nice bookshop with comfy chairs, later emerging with the new release by Gabriel García Márquez. Flip had heard somewhere that, before García Márquez died, he'd requested that this manuscript be destroyed. The dementia he'd experienced while writing it had been bad enough to affect his writing, but he was still lucid enough to recognize the work as sub-par. His sons, however, had published it anyway.

If Flip dropped dead right now, his unfinished novel would die too, but unlike García Márquez, he didn't have a zillion fans who would be devastated by the loss. In fact, the only ones who would be upset were his publishers, who'd never recoup his advance.

What would happen to his current books in print and to incoming royalties? He had no idea. No will. No next of kin. The only people he was truly on speaking terms with nowadays were his agent and editor, and if he didn't finish that damned manuscript, they'd stop talking to him too.

By the time he returned to St. Philip Street, he was footsore and exhausted. His intention was to go up to his apartment and take a nap before finding a late dinner nearby. The world—and the book—could wait another day.

As he fumbled in his phone for the code that unlocked the door to the building—he was shit at remembering numbers—someone called from across the street. "Hey! You!"

He twisted and saw that it was the fortune teller who'd set up a cloth-covered card table and two chairs under a gallery. He'd nodded to her during his trips in and out today but hadn't otherwise interacted. She was in her sixties, he'd guess, her pale skin deeply lined, her short hair dyed several neon colors, her nose sporting both a ring and a stud.

"Hey! Tall boy!"

"Yeah?"

"Come 'ere."

"Thanks, but I don't need my fortune told."

"Good. 'Cause I ain't gonna tell it." She gestured him forward.

It was bound to be some kind of scam, or maybe it was just general craziness in action. But she seemed dead set on getting him over there, and he was curious why. Flip crossed the street and, as directed, sat across from her. The sign on the table identified her as Miss Amelie.

She didn't say anything as she gave him a close visual inspection. He figured he might as well do the same, and they peered at each other for several moments. He upped his age estimate into the seventies and noted the sharp alertness in her eyes. He was willing to bet that nothing much got past this woman.

"How long you plannin' to stay?" she finally asked, lighting a cigarette.

"I don't—"

"You moved in yesterday." She pointed up at his gallery across the street. "When you gonna leave?"

He scowled at her. "Look, I've signed a valid rental agreement. I have every right to—"

"Ain't tryin' to scare you off, boy. Just wanna know some things about my new neighbor."

Did that mean she lived there too? If so, she had an

easy commute to work. "Sorry," he said. "I'm just kinda tired and grouchy. Moving's a pain and—"

"Especially if you ain't got your suitcase." Smirking, she took a long drag. "Don't look so goggle-eyed, boy. I'm a seer, remember."

More like a hearer, he decided after a pause. He'd had his windows open while talking to the airline today, and the sound must have carried down to her. "In answer to your question: three months." He'd been able to budget that much. After that, he'd have to find a day job or move somewhere with cheaper rent. But those were things to worry about later.

Miss Amelie stroked her chin. "Three months, huh?"

"Is that a problem?"

"A challenge more like." She cackled, and he didn't understand why. Then she waved her hand, indicating the items on her table: a deck of tarot cards, a pair of golden dice, and an old-fashioned illustration of a human palm. "You see all this? It's bullshit."

"Um... okay."

"I just use 'em 'cause folks expect 'em. Truth is, I don't need no cards or nothing to divinate. I just see things here." She tapped the center of her forehead. "My Clear Eye is wide open. Always has been."

He knew he should simply humor her, but he couldn't help shaking his head. "If you can foresee things, how come you're not rich and famous?"

Instead of being offended, she laughed loudly. "You think I want to be them things? I'm happy right here, boy. And anyway, my Eye don't let me see lottery numbers or shit like that. I can't tell nobody what stocks to buy or which side to bet on. I just *see* shit. It's a knowin'. I can't control it. Dunno if I would even if I could. Seems shifty to me, tryin' to stay three jumps ahead of anyone else."

They watched a mule-drawn carriage slowly roll by, the mule's hooves clomping on the pavement and the tourists goggling at Flip and Miss Amelie. The carriage driver, who had a tiny dog next to him, waved, and Miss Amelie waved back.

"Your Clear Eye's wide open too, you know," she said to Flip after the carriage turned the corner.

He instinctively touched his forehead, but of course all he felt was skin. "I doubt that."

"'Course it is. How else would you be able to write your stories? You *see* those people you write about even if they don't exactly exist."

"That's not how—" Flip stopped himself because, in truth, he had no explanation for where his stories came from. They just sort of appeared in his brain like gifts from a muse, and they felt as real as anything else around him. Sometimes more real; he'd been accused more than once of living in his head.

Well, if he did have some kind of magic eye, it was squeezed shut now. He hadn't been able to envision his story at all.

And how did she know he was an author? More eavesdropping? Had she spoken with his landlord, whom Flip had yet to meet in person?

Miss Amelie stubbed out her cigarette on an amber glass ashtray. "You know, that building you're livin' in, it's over two hundred years old. Imagine all the folks who've been inside those walls, all the things that have happened. Imagine what a boy with his Eye open could see in there." She gave an enigmatic smile.

For no valid reason, Flip shivered. "If you're trying to get me scared of ghosts, it's not going to happen."

"Don't need to be scared of none of the ghosts 'round here. Ain't no bad ones in *my* neighborhood."

"That's reassuring."

She moved her hand in the direction of his apartment. "Get on home now, Phillip. It's fixin' to rain."

The sky did look ominous; he hadn't noticed that before. He stood. "It was good to meet you, Miss Amelie. I guess I'll be seeing you around."

"You'll be seeing lots of things." And she cackled.

The first raindrops fell moments after he entered his apartment, as he was taking off his shoes. By the time he went to the window and looked out, water was sheeting down impressively. The sidewalk and gallery across the street were empty, with no sign of Miss Amelie, although he had no idea how she'd been able to pack up so quickly.

He meandered to the desk and sat down. There was that taunting cursor, blinking away at him. Since it couldn't hurt, he took a few deep breaths and pictured a closed eyelid in the center of his forehead, then imagined it slowly opening to reveal an eye. Hazel like his real ones, but bigger and with infinitely better vision. He—

Wait. Had Miss Amelie called him Phillip? How the hell did she know his name?

Even as he tried to pursue that line of thought, however, his hands rose to the keyboard and began to type. For the first time in weeks, he saw his story.

It was past two in the morning when Flip finally climbed into his enormous bed, setting down his phone without even bothering to check the whereabouts of his suitcase. He'd written over four thousand words tonight, a huge daily number for him and more than he'd managed in all of the preceding weeks. Not only that, but the next scenes had already crystallized and he'd made some notes to remember them. He'd only stopped writing because his vision was getting too blurry.

Rain still fell but more softly, pattering against the street and the buildings' exteriors. There wasn't much else in the way of noise at this hour. In the darkness, aboard his huge bed, Flip easily imagined himself afloat on a calm sea, thousands of miles from his troubles. He let the pretend waves carry him straight into sleep.

And, as it turned out, into a dream.

THREE

Scratch leaned against the wall near the door, watching Flip, who sat on the edge of the bed. It was dark outside; the only light inside the room came from a pair of lanterns that flanked the door. The flickering flames sent shadows dancing on the walls, and although the shadows looked disconcertingly like people, they didn't frighten Flip. Nor did Scratch, in the same suit as last night but with a different tie and pocket square.

"What are you doing on that little computer of yours?" Scratch asked.

"Writing a novel."

Scratch whistled. "We got us a writer. Nice. I like the click-clack of typewriters better, though. They're like music." He spread his hands and moved his fingers as if typing—or playing a piano—and hummed a tune that Flip didn't recognize.

"I'm not musical."

"Nah, everyone's got music in them somewhere. You just haven't found yours, is all." Scratch tilted his hat at a more rakish angle and winked.

"I don't need music. I need my luggage." Flip sighed dramatically and fell back onto the bed. The dream's ceiling was festooned with dusty spiderwebs, certainly not true in real life, and the shadows were especially lively up there. They looked like human figures moving around, but he couldn't make out what they were doing.

The mattress dipped slightly as Scratch sat beside him. "Back, oh, 'bout a hundred and fifty years ago, this was a tenement house. A whole family would live in this one room. Hot summer nights, they'd sleep out on the gallery, getting sucked dry by mosquitoes while hoping for a cooling breeze."

Maybe Flip had read this somewhere about his building, or maybe his subconscious had created the story out of whole cloth. "I'm going to be gone from here before it gets too hot."

"Where will you go?"

"No fucking idea." Flip decided it was stupid to spend a dream lying flat, so he sat up and turned to look at Scratch. "Honestly, it's kinda weird, not knowing what I'm going to do. I used to have plans."

Looking wistful, Scratch removed his hat and moved it around in his hands. His soft brown curls were cut short and oiled into place. "I did too," he said softly.

"What were they?" Flip was curious to see what his dreaming mind would come up with.

"Well, they weren't very specific plans. But... a little more fun. And I was saving money from my job—I was a piano player at a house in Storyville, and sometimes I worked at my cousin's coffeehouse too, only there I poured liquor. I figured someday soon I'd buy myself a little Creole cottage. Maybe even marry some nice girl and have some kids."

Interesting. Flip hadn't realized his subconscious harbored picket-fence hopes. "And did your plans come true?"

Scratch gave him a level look. "Nah, man. But look, it ain't too late for you. You can—"

"It's not too late for you either."

That brought wry laughter. "It's hard to start a family when you're dead."

Flip blinked at him.

The shadows on the ceiling stopped moving, as if they were listening to the conversation, and the room filled with the cloying scent of flowers. Flip shivered, wrapped his arms around himself, and chewed his lip. There was a truth in this dream, if only he could grasp it.

"I'm a ghost." Scratch's voice was matter-of-fact but his eyes held a deep sorrow.

"I don't believe in ghosts."

"Doesn't matter whether you believe—we're here. More of us than living folks. People have been dying in this place for hundreds of years, and not all of us pass on."

Flip had never had much interest in spiritual or supernatural matters. The books he read and the books he wrote were solidly grounded in reality, which he figured was plenty damned weird enough. It must have been today's encounter with Miss Amelie that got him thinking about the uncanny.

"But most do pass on?" he asked.

"Sure. Don't ask me where they go, 'cause I don't know. Ain't been there myself."

In response to Flip's stare, Scratch snorted, stood, and crossed to the French doors. He pushed one of the curtains aside, swung the door open, and gestured for Flip to join him. After a moment's hesitation, Flip obeyed, and they stood side by side on the gallery, looking down at the empty street. It was no longer raining, although the pavement was still wet. Faint voices carried from somewhere in the distance.

But then Flip realized that the street wasn't empty at all. People were on the move, some on foot, some in horse-drawn wagons. A few pushed carts. There were cars as well, including a Model T Ford and a tail-finned Chevy, and somehow they weren't running over the slower-moving people and vehicles. The people wore a huge variety of clothing, including decorated skins and robes, multilayer outfits that during the wearers' lives must have felt sweltering, crinoline-supported skirts, and punk regalia.

Aside from the mishmash of time, there was

nothing remarkable about the scene. The passersby were simply going about their everyday lives. Or... non-lives, as the case might be.

"I thought being a ghost would be more exciting," Flip said as he watched a young man in bell-bottom jeans crouch to tie his shoe.

Scratch shrugged. "It can be, sometimes."

"So how old were you when you died?"

"A week past my thirtieth birthday. Too old to be tomcattin' around, my mama said." He was almost breathtakingly handsome when he grinned like that.

"And how did you die?"

"Murdered. Right here in this room."

Flip glanced into the apartment, as if he might glimpse a gory scene, but there was no sign of a corpse. "You don't sound very upset about it."

"I've gotten past the grief—it was over a hundred years ago. Anyway, I sort of had it coming. Man caught me in bed with his wife. Which I guess he might have dealt with less violently, except a few nights earlier I'd been in bed with *him*." There was that smile again. "In my defense, I didn't know they were married to each other. If I had, I'd have suggested something cozy for all three of us."

Great. Bisexual polyamorous ghosts. What the *hell* was going on in Flip's brain?

He wandered back inside and sat on the bed. He was tired, which was nonsensical since he was asleep. But he'd never had a dream like this before, one that went on for so long with such depth of detail and logical clarity. One that felt so real.

After a few minutes, Scratch returned and sat beside him. "I miss getting drunk," Scratch said. "Booze led me to a lot of wrong places, but I sure did enjoy the ride."

"I'm not much of a drinker." Flip had seen early in life what alcohol did to his parents, and he very much wanted to avoid the same fate.

"Fair enough." Scratch sighed. "And I miss... being touched. Being a ghost is a lonely thing."

Well, he was handsome, and he seemed sad, and this was all imaginary anyhow, so what the hell. Flip settled a hand on Scratch's knee. They both looked at it, the skin pale against the dark fabric.

"Ah," said Scratch in a honeyed tone, "so you're inclined that way. That's a stroke of luck for me." He tossed his hat to the floor and twisted to face Flip, and goddamn, he was beautiful.

So Flip kissed him.

Scratch gasped and drew back, eyes wide. "You can kiss me!"

"I, uh... yeah. You didn't want me to?" Flip wasn't sure how consent worked with dream figments; maybe he should have asked first.

"No, I want. Nobody's been able to do that before. Not in any of the dreams I've visited. I can flirt, sometimes they flirt back, but...." Hesitantly, he brushed his fingers over Flip's mouth, sending pleasant shivers down Flip's spine.

This time Scratch initiated the kiss. He was somehow both tender and ravenous, cradling Flip's face in his palms and pressing their lips together, easing his tongue in, stealing all of Flip's oxygen. Scratch tasted of cigarettes and bourbon, a flavor that Flip found unexpectedly delicious. All of Scratch was delicious: his warm lips, his strong hands, the delighted little moans he made. Even his oiled hair felt good between Flip's fingers.

"Whoo!" said Scratch after they'd separated to catch their breath. "That was something. I don't remember kissing being that good."

"Me either." Maybe kisses never had been that good in real life. Certainly none of them had ever made his head swim the way it did now, or made his cock so achingly hard.

Scratch stared solemnly at him, then licked his own lips. "I could taste you. Mint."

"Toothpaste."

"Y'know, most of the time I don't mind too much being a ghost. I can still listen to music and watch people doing their things. I get gossip from other ghosts, so I know what's going on around town. I don't feel sorry for myself. But another person's touch— that's one of the things that makes a body feel alive, ain't it? Kissing, petting, fucking... I liked doing those things a *lot* 'cause when I did, I felt so strong, so vital. A taste of immortality." He gave a soft laugh. "But just a taste. And now you've given me that again. Thank you." He lifted one of Flip's hands and kissed the back of it.

Then he stood, put on his hat, and left the room, closing the door softly behind him.

Flip expected to wake up then, but he didn't. Instead he lay back on the bed, chasing the lingering flavors on his tongue as he watched the shadows. Outside, hooves clip-clopped on the pavement, although it was too late for the tourist carriages to be out. Occasional voices wafted in, but he couldn't make out what they were saying. If he strained his ears, he could hear a piano playing a tune he didn't recognize—something old-fashioned, like in a saloon in a Western movie.

He lay there and thought about plans left unfulfilled.

IN THE MORNING, his AirTag tracker said his suitcase was in Atlanta, although the airline rep insisted that it was on the way to New Orleans. He hoped the damned thing was having a fun adventure.

He had beignets for breakfast, just like a tourist, but not at Café du Monde because, as usual, the line was ridiculously long. He called a cab and rode to the nearest Target, on the other side of the river, to buy socks, underwear, and T-shirts, along with a few household goods. He was still going to need a couple pairs of jeans and a shirt or two, but those could wait for another excursion. Maybe some thrift store visits would be a good idea if he hoped to stretch his budget.

When he returned to St. Philip Street, Miss Amelie was sitting in her usual spot. She waved at him.

"Morning," he called. He couldn't wave because his hands were full of bags.

"Smart move, goin' shoppin'. You ain't gonna see your suitcase again soon."

"Did you see that in the cards?"

"Nah, I just know airlines." She cackled and then coughed. "But if you go see my friend Marie-Louise over on Mandeville Street, she could make you a gris-gris. A charm. Might help. Couldn't hurt."

"I'll keep that in mind, thanks." He would have rather had a voodoo doll of the airline CEO, but asking for that was probably culturally insensitive.

He wrote about a thousand words and, feeling accomplished, ate a sandwich and decided to take a walk. He couldn't afford to join a gym and he hated jogging, so walking and going up and down his apartment stairs were going to be his best forms of exercise.

But he'd traveled only a couple of blocks before pausing in front of a mansion.

Bergeron-Catanzaro House

Tours Available on the Hour

A glance at his watch told him it was five minutes before two. *Well, why not?* He walked through the front door and into a long, wide hallway with ornate rugs and a trio of chandeliers.

A young woman inside the first room on the left

was spreading a cloth onto a long folding table. "Oh, hello," she said brightly. "Are you here for a tour?"

"Yes, please."

"Hang on just a sec." She poked at her phone. "Tony'll be right here. Sorry—I usually do the tours, but I need to finish setting up here. Tomorrow we have the St. Joseph altar."

He nodded as if he knew what that meant.

Flip returned to the hallway, which could have qualified as a substantial room on its own. At the far end, opposite where he had entered the house, a transom-topped door led outside. Large paintings of sailing ships and craggy mountains hung on the side walls and, below them, a few narrow tables held vases, brochures, and knickknacks. There were several doorways along either side of the hall, some with open doors, others closed.

When a figure stepped out from the farthest room on the right, Flip nearly cried out.

The man looked like Scratch.

CHAPTER

FOUR

"Hey, are you okay?" The man was heading down the long hallway toward Flip, who was, in fact, light-headed and weak-kneed.

By the time the man reached him, Flip had managed to regain a bit of composure. "I'm fine. Sorry. I think I just got walloped by jet lag." That wasn't a particularly good excuse, but it would have to do.

The man's nervous expression eased into a smile. "And this city can be a little overwhelming sometimes. Anyway, welcome. I'm Anthony Bergeron. Tony, actually. Assistant director. And you're here for the tour?"

"Yes, please."

"Great! Let me talk to Kat for just a sec and then we can get started."

"It's just me?" Flip was surprised.

"Unless someone else shows up in the next three minutes, you get me all to yourself. Hang on."

Tony ducked into the nearby room to talk to the young woman, which gave Flip a good opportunity to stare at him. Of course, he wasn't dressed like Scratch; instead of a suit, Tony wore jeans and a pale-blue oxford shirt. His hair was the same dark brown as Scratch's, but unoiled so that the curls were more noticeable. He had the same face shape, high cheekbones, and somewhat pointy chin. The same sensual lips, strong nose, and arched brows. His height and build were identical to Scratch's. He even moved with the same confident grace and gave the same overall impression of a man assured of his own beauty and determined not to take life too seriously. The biggest difference between them were the eyes—dark amber for both of them, but Tony's lacked the depths of sorrow that sometimes appeared in Scratch's gaze.

And, of course, Tony was entirely real, whereas Scratch was a dream ghost.

There was a logical explanation for the resemblance—there had to be. Either Flip was misremembering what Scratch looked like, or he'd passed Tony on the street. Flip lived only two blocks away from here, after all, and even a brief encounter could have influenced his dreams.

But neither of those explanations rang true.

He was pulled out of his reverie by Tony, back in the hallway and smiling at him. "Looks like you get a private tour. Usually we charge ten bucks, but a couple of the rooms are sort of a mess right now because we just finished an art exhibition, so I'm not going to charge you. Your house tour is on the house."

Oh, that wink was *exactly* like Scratch.

"That's really nice of you. I hope I'm not keeping you from more important work."

"Giving tours is my favorite thing, and I don't often get to do it. So let me formally welcome you to the Bergeron-Catanzaro House, built in 1826 and named after two of the families that lived here."

Rather belatedly, Flip had a realization. "Bergeron. That's your—"

"Yep. Sadly, my family hasn't owned this place since the mid-nineteenth century. But I credit the house with giving me a career. When I was a kid, my parents used to point it out and tell me it was ours once, and that got me interested in our family history, and *that* got me interested in history in general. Then a job opened up here right after I finished my MA and... and, I'm sorry, you didn't come here for the Anthony Bergeron Life Story." He looked a little sheepish but not truly regretful.

"It's a good story. I'm glad you told me. That connection is really cool."

"C'mon. Let me show you around the place."

The tour started in a large front room that had begun life as a parlor or music room. Tony launched into an explanation of who built the house and why it was designed the way it was. His tale continued as they peeked into a bedroom, a bathroom—obviously not original to the house—a dining room, a kitchen, and a long window-lined space that he said had once been the site of an organized-crime-related shootout. Although the stories themselves were interesting, what really delighted Flip was Tony's depth of knowledge and passion for his subject.

The tour was thorough and not simply confined to the main house. Together they explored the courtyard, the gardens, and the building that had originally housed the kitchen and enslaved people. Tony didn't try to underplay the grimness of slavery. As they stood in the lower part of that building, which had been used as an office by the man who owned the place in the 1950s, Tony spread his hands. "Some people like to argue that it was better to be a slave working in a fine house rather than in the sugarcane fields, and maybe that's so, but the truth is that these people were forced to work hard, tolerate substandard housing, and endure assaults on their dignity, autonomy, and physical safety."

Flip nodded. He could never hope to truly understand what enslaved people had gone through, but seeing a place where some of them had lived helped make their stories feel more real to him. "I have no clue whether any of my ancestors owned other human beings. Does it make you feel weird to know that yours did?"

Luckily, Tony didn't seem offended by the question. "A little, yeah. But also, some of my ancestors *were* enslaved. I'm New Orleans Creole. My people came from France, Spain, Africa, Haiti, Sicily. I'm not proud of everything they all did. But it's complicated, you know? Anyway, I guess if you go digging around in *anyone*'s family history, you're going to unearth some hard truths."

"Wouldn't have to dig far with me," Flip muttered. One generation would do it.

By the time they returned to the hallway near the front door, over ninety minutes had passed, a half hour longer than the official tour. Apparently nobody had shown up for the three o'clock, which was just fine with Flip. He'd enjoyed his time with Tony. "Well, thanks," he said, feeling a little awkward. "A lot, I mean. This was great."

Tony beamed. "How long are you in town? I can recommend some places to visit if you want to absorb more history. Or, you know, just eat well." Was that a slightly flirty tone? Maybe.

"Oh, I live here, actually. I mean, I just moved here two days ago. I'm just a couple blocks away." Flip pointed in the direction of his apartment.

"That's great! I—" Tony paused, a blush coloring his cheeks. "Um, it's a great city. Lots to see and do."

It had been a long time since Flip had flirted back with someone. Eons. But Tony was so handsome and charming, and Flip felt as if they'd known each other much longer than ninety minutes. "I'd love to hear your suggestions."

Their gazes caught. Flip had to squash the irrational and idiotic urge to pull Tony into a kiss. It didn't help when Tony's tongue darted out to briefly lick his bottom lip.

"Tell you what." Tony glanced around as if someone might be listening in and then dropped his voice to nearly a whisper. "I'm tied up tonight and tomorrow, but how about if we meet here Thursday around two o'clock? I have the afternoon off, and I'll take you on a walking tour of the French Quarter. Also free of charge," he added with a grin.

Flip decided to be brave. "I could take us out to dinner. Just to be fair."

"I like that plan very much."

Plan. That word renewed Flip's memory of Scratch, but he pushed the thought away. It was dumb to be thinking of imaginary men when he'd soon be going on a date with a real one.

"Hey," Tony added, almost as an afterthought, "I never asked your name."

"Flip Devin. No houses named after me, as far as I know."

"See you Thursday, Flip Devin."

HE WROTE MORE words that evening and sketchily plotted out the next several scenes. His suitcase, he learned, was now in Houston. If he could bring himself to believe the airline rep, it was due to arrive in New Orleans first thing in the morning.

When it was fairly late, he took a stroll down

Bourbon Street, where drunken, noisy crowds still swarmed, and the music and bright lights swirled around him like a fever dream. Sometimes he thought he saw, out of the corner of his eye, a woman dressed in a long gown or a man in a stovepipe hat, but they always disappeared when he turned his head to look. The odors of booze, perfume, tobacco and marijuana smoke, and frying food filled his nose. He remembered watching *Dumbo* when he was a little kid, intrigued but also frightened by the scene in which the little elephant gets drunk and hallucinates. Now he was Dumbo, despite being sober.

He fell asleep shortly after returning home, and he didn't dream.

In the morning, an airline rep very earnestly told him that his luggage piece was on the way to New Orleans, while the AirTag said it was back in Oakland. "Can I at least get frequent flyer miles for all the travel my suitcase has done?" he asked the rep. She wasn't amused.

Guided by his phone, he walked a couple of miles to a vintage clothing shop. It had higher prices than a thrift store, but he found a couple of shirts he liked, including a collared sweater with an orange-and-brown geometric design. The sweater, he thought, would be perfect for tomorrow's date with Tony. If it was a date. It might be just a friendly local showing a newcomer around. And the sweater would be fine for that as well.

Afterward he gathered more groceries and returned

home to write. It was warm today—and far muggier than California—and although he initially produced a lot of words, torpor eventually settled in. He stripped out of his sweaty clothes and lay spread-eagled on the bed, thankful for the ceiling fan. For some reason it was easier to believe in ghosts, fortunetelling, and the third eye when heat clung to the skin and made the air feel thick and blurry.

Miss Amelie was across the street when, freshly showered, he ventured out for dinner. "Told you," she called. "Open up that Clear Eye and the writing flows nice and easy. Never mind the heat. You'll get used to it."

Could she see him at his desk, typing away? He didn't think the angle was right for that. Maybe she lived in an apartment across the way and could spy on him from there.

Flip strolled over to her. "How long have you lived around here?"

She frowned in thought. "In the Quarter? Moved here after Katrina. But I've lived in the city my whole life."

"I can't imagine that. I've never lived anywhere for more than a few years."

"You ain't found the right garden to put down your roots. Don't mean you won't. But some folks don't get planted until they die." She gave a raspy laugh.

He wasn't sure how he felt about that. He used to think that he was content being a tumbleweed, to use her plant analogy. He'd thought it meant freedom.

Lately, though, he was maybe feeling untethered in a more negative way. Unconnected to anywhere—or to anyone.

Miss Amelie shuffled a deck of cards but didn't deal any of them out. "You think you came here because you had fun on vacation in this city once, and 'cause it ain't cold here in March, and 'cause you figure it's a good city for authors. But maybe you came here 'cause you're s'posed to be here." She leaned back in the chair, her expression implying she'd said something significant.

Flip felt slightly stunned. Her analysis of his reasons was spot-on. But he didn't agree with her last sentence. "Are you talking about fate? I don't believe in fate."

She harrumphed and slammed down the deck of cards. "Don't believe in ghosts, don't believe in fate. What *do* you believe in, boy? Anyhow, that ain't what I meant. Sometimes a person just fits into a particular place like a piece of a jigsaw puzzle. Could be 'cause they got ties there, or could be they're just the right shape. Now, get along and find yourself dinner. Turn left when you get to Decatur and go up a block to the place with the duck quesadillas. That's what you're in the mood for. And hurry yourself or you're gonna get caught in the rain."

He'd never even heard of a duck quesadilla, but now that she'd mentioned it, well, it sounded pretty tasty. His stomach growled. "See you later, Miss Amelie."

She was staring down at her phone and didn't look up. "Tell that old player that I wouldn't mind if he came around again. Ain't seen him for a long time."

Flip decided it was best not to ask what she meant by this—and even better not to think about it at all. He shook his head and headed for Decatur.

The restaurant wasn't anything fancy, but the quesadillas hit the spot perfectly. Flip sat at the bar to eat, enjoying the noisy buzz of conversations and the bustle of activity, even when people bumped into him in passing. He was just considering whether he might still be hungry enough for red beans and rice when there was a loud crash. Momentarily startled, he recovered and identified it as a thunderclap. Miss Amelie had said that rain was on the way, but of course nobody needed supernatural talents to foresee the weather. They could just use a phone app.

Flip decided to forgo the extra food, and by the time he stepped onto the sidewalk, several more thunderclaps had resounded and large drops were starting to pelt the pavement. He took off for home at a fast clip, grateful he had only a few blocks to travel. Rain started sheeting down in earnest before he turned the corner onto St. Philip, leaving him soaked to the skin. Water flowed down the streets as if they were rivers, carrying wrappers and other bits of debris. He thought he saw a crowd of people hurrying northwest, away from the river, but that must have been some odd trick of the downpour and poor light, because when he squinted he saw that the street was empty.

Just outside the door to his building, a mangled umbrella lay on the pavement like a dead prehistoric bird. It was the kind with a handle you could hook over your arm when it wasn't raining. Without really thinking about it, he picked the thing up and closed it as best he could—which wasn't very well—and carried it inside. He stood for a moment in the building's small vestibule, dripping and staring bemusedly at the broken umbrella.

And damned if he didn't carry the umbrella upstairs to his apartment and set it in the corner of the kitchen, as if it might possibly be useful for something. He didn't feel quite right in the head. Not insane, but... muddled. It was as if he had a high fever, except he didn't feel sick at all. Or maybe it was like being drunk or high. No, that wasn't it. He felt as if he were in a dream. Hell, his *actual* dreams—the ones with Scratch —had felt more real than he did now.

Dazed, he wandered out onto the gallery, where the rain fell so hard that he could barely breathe, where he was blind to everything but the bolts of lightning and the thunder that reverberated through his body like an alien heartbeat. He heard a piano playing something lively, and a crowd laughing. He tasted cigarettes and bourbon.

When he came inside, he closed the windows but not the curtains, stripped off every stitch of clothing, and sat down to write.

Flip didn't notice when the storm ended. He didn't notice anything outside the world of his story until his eyesight grew so fuzzy that he could barely read the screen. He gasped when he saw his word count. Seven thousand words. He'd never written anywhere near that many in one day, but tonight they'd flowed effortlessly, as fast as runoff rain gushing through a downspout.

He gathered his still-damp clothing from the floor and carried it into the bathroom, where he tossed it into the tub. He'd deal with it in the morning. Still naked, and after a minimum of nighttime ablutions, he climbed into bed.

"I like how the rain cleans the streets," said Scratch, holding and toying with the folded umbrella.

Flip sat up and blinked rapidly. He hadn't even realized he was falling asleep, but now here Scratch was, sitting on the edge of the mattress and grinning at him. Scratch wore charcoal trousers, a white shirt, and a striped tie, as usual, but tonight he didn't have a vest or jacket or hat.

"We don't usually get big thunderstorms on the West Coast," said Flip.

"That's right. You're from California." He drew the name of the state out, making it sound exotic. Then he cocked his head and stared at Flip's bare chest. "Y'all don't wear pajamas in California?"

"Sometimes."

"My mama used to remind me to wear something decent to bed. 'What if there's a fire in the middle of the night?' she used to say. 'Y'all want the neighborhood to see you in all your glory?'"

"Did you follow her advice?"

"Depends on whether I had company. I figured if there was a fire and there were two of us with no clothes on, folks wouldn't know which of us to stare at." His smile faded. "There's a lot more she said that I should have listened to. Mama's been dead now for a long time, but she outlived me. I caused her and my daddy so much grief."

"Are they ghosts too?"

"Nah. How about you? Do you do what your mama tells you?"

That made Flip squirm. "I haven't talked to her in years. And even when we were in touch, she wasn't much for imparting guidance."

"Sorry to hear that. You have other relatives you can lean on when you need it?"

Flip shook his head.

"Sorry to hear that too. I got—well, I *had*—a big family. Aunts and uncles, brothers and sisters, cousins. I could hardly do anything without one of them noticing and reporting back to my parents, even after I was fully grown. But they were all there for me whenever I got myself in a bind. Up 'til that last time, that is. None of them could help me when I got shot." He looked down at his chest, where a crimson stain suddenly bloomed like a terrible flower.

Flip cried out in alarm and the blood disappeared.

Scratch patted Flip's blanket-covered knee. "Sorry 'bout that." Then he set the umbrella on the floor with great care, as if it were valuable, and twisted around to face Flip more directly. "What'd you do today besides writing?"

"Shopped. Ate. Walked."

"I used to walk a lot too. Partly out of necessity—didn't have no car back then—but I also liked it. I miss it. Wish I could see what the rest of the city looks like now."

"Why can't you?"

"Can't go more than a couple blocks from the spot where I died." Scratch raised his eyebrows and spread his arms, his message clear. He'd died right *here*.

It wasn't something that Flip wanted to think about, so he changed the subject. "I've been taking a lot of photos during my walks. Want to see them?"

Joy illuminated Scratch's face and made his eyes sparkle. "Can I?"

So Flip lifted his phone off the nightstand and gestured for Scratch to sit beside him, both of them with backs against the headboard and legs stretched out straight, Flip under the blanket and Scratch above. Flip scrolled slowly through his recent pictures. Sometimes he paused to explain something, but other times it was Scratch who explained. "That's Congo Square. I used to go there on Sundays to listen to the bands," and "My sister, Delphine? Her husband's people are in that cemetery. Dunno if she ended up there too," and "That restaurant was around in my time too. One of my cousins waited tables there."

Flip wondered about the accuracy of some of the details Scratch shared. Maybe those things were true, and Flip had heard or read about them at some point and then forgot. Or maybe his subconscious was simply creating plausible fictions. That's what he did for a living, after all.

In any case, it was an enjoyable experience, with Scratch pressed against his side and clearly delighted with the photos, and with Flip's head feeling clearer than it had all day.

When they ran out of recent photos, Scratch took control of the phone and started scrolling backward. "No wonder you people spend so much time on these things. Hey, who's this?"

Flip fought the impulse to snatch the phone away. "Nobody."

"Don't look like nobody. Two of you are scrunched up together and all smiles."

"That's… my ex."

Flip had taken the selfie six months ago, when the shadows were already deepening but he was still hoping for a happy resolution. Flip's newest book had just released, and he and Ethan had celebrated with a weekend getaway to Catalina Island. The picture had been taken on the ferry ride over. They had a big argument just a few hours later and both spent the rest of the weekend sulking, playing on their phones and barely speaking to each other.

"I'm better looking," Scratch announced.

"Agreed."

"What happened to him?"

Flip shrugged. "Nothing. As far as I know, he's still in Oakland. He probably has a new boyfriend. Maybe Ethan's cheating on him too."

With a derisive snort, Scratch set the phone screen-down on the nightstand. "I never did that… exactly. Mostly I didn't make any promises. Not to the fellow who killed me and not to his wife. Only slept with each of them once. Not even once with the wife, really. Bastard killed me while we were in flagrante. He could've just joined us instead and then we'd all three of us been happy."

"Well, Ethan did. Cheat, I mean." But he might as well be honest, at least in his dreams. "I wasn't entirely blameless."

"You cheated too?"

"No. But I didn't treat him all that well, and when he tried to talk to me about it, I just shut him out. Story of my life." He'd seen a therapist for a while, a few years back, who thought that Flip might be pushing people away before they had a chance to reject him. Maybe so—probably the result of shithead parents and a fucked-up childhood—and it was possible that a whole lot of counseling and effort might have improved him. But Flip had bailed on the therapist too.

"Bad decisions, huh?" Scratch's smile looked sympathetic.

"Yeah. One of many."

"Least yours didn't get you shot."

He had a point.

They sat there together, watching the ceiling fan spin, each lost in his own thoughts. Except Scratch wasn't lost in anything because he was just a figment; Flip needed to remember that. It was difficult to do, though, when he heard Scratch breathing—did ghosts need to breathe?—and felt the slight pressure of Scratch's shoulder against his.

Anyway, it was surprisingly nice, just relaxing in silent company. They'd each traveled very different roads, but they could share these moments.

Except Scratch wasn't real, dammit.

Although he sure felt real when he took Flip's hand in his and kissed his knuckles. "You got long fingers," Scratch said. "Like a piano player." He stretched out his free hand as illustration.

"Well, I do play a computer keyboard."

Scratch chuckled and bumped their shoulders together. "You know," he said after a pause, "that kiss was mighty nice."

"It was."

"And you don't have any clothes on, and I could also not have any clothes on, and...." He sighed deeply. "It's been so long, Flip."

"It's been a dry spell for me too. Which is probably why I'm dreaming you."

"You're dreaming me 'cause I'm here," said Scratch. "And how long has your dry spell been? 'Cause mine's lasted for a century."

Four months suddenly didn't seem like so long.

While Flip was still considering this, Scratch did a gymnastic feat and was suddenly straddling Flip, torso bent forward so their lips could meet. This kiss was even better than the first, because now they knew each other a little better, and Flip was naked, and their groins were in contact despite several layers of cloth between them. And Scratch had a true talent for this, knowing exactly how to alternate between delicate brushes against tender skin, hungry invasions with his tongue, and teasing little nips along jawline and down the neck.

"Thought... you were a ghost... not a vampire," Flip panted. He had his hands planted firmly on Scratch's hips, holding him in place.

Scratch merely hummed a laugh and began working his way down Flip's chest. When he bit playfully at a nipple, Flip nearly lost his mind.

Things would have proceeded very quickly from that point, except Flip remembered his plans for the following afternoon and froze.

"Something wrong, baby?" Scratch looked concerned.

"I think we should stop. Uh, maybe."

"Maybe? It seems like you're feeling good." Scratch did a little wiggle that ground his ass against Flip's very hard cock, making Flip groan. "Real good."

Realizing that he was still holding Scratch against him, Flip let go and spread his arms wide. It wasn't an easy thing to do. He wanted every inch of Scratch pressed tightly against him. "I'm trying to decide if this counts as cheating," he admitted.

"With Ethan?"

"No, he's absolutely past-tense for me. But tomorrow I have a date—well, I'm not sure if it's technically a date, but it's at least a close cousin of one—with a man I met yesterday. He's going to show me around town. He's a historian," he added, as if that were somehow relevant.

Scratch's face registered amusement. "Did you tell him that you wouldn't go near another man?"

"Of course not. And anyway, I haven't. You're not even real."

"I may be dead, but I'm as real as you are." Scratch poked Flip hard in the belly.

"I'm dreaming you."

"I'm *in* your dream, but that's... it just makes things easier, is all." Scratch heaved a loud sigh and rolled off of Flip, then stood on the floor. "But I don't fool around with nobody unless they're into it, and I guess you ain't."

"I am. I was. I just...." Flip made a garbled sound of frustration and covered his face with a pillow.

When he tossed the pillow aside, Scratch was still there, looking down at him with the corner of his mouth quirked. His tie was loose and his shirt rumpled; his hair had started to escape the oil or pomade or whatever he used, and soft curls were beginning to take over. He looked even more handsome when disheveled.

"Sorry," said Flip. "You're sort of hard up, and I'm not making any sense."

"Feelings are feelings. And I've never wanted anyone to regret what we've done together. I still feel bad about the fellow who shot me and the woman I was in bed with at the time." He brightened. "Tell you what. How about some music? That always improves my mood, and I ain't played for nobody in a long time."

"But how—" Flip stopped abruptly because there was a piano in one corner of the room. It wasn't there in real life and hadn't existed in his dream until now, but there it was. "Um, okay."

Scratch sat at the piano, interlaced his hands to crack his knuckles, and gave his shoulders a shake as if to loosen them up. Then he began to play a lively tune that put Flip in mind of young women with bobbed hair and short, fringed dresses kicking up their heels.

He was good, and Flip couldn't help wiggling his toes and swaying along with him.

When Scratch finished, Flip clapped, and Scratch gave a little seated bow. "It's called *After You're Gone*. It was a big hit the year I died. I used to play it a lot. The year before, the military closed down the brothels in Storyville, so I was kinda hard up for musical work, but I found it now and then."

"I don't know anything about jazz, but I liked that song. Will you play another?"

Clearly pleased, Scratch put his fingers on the keys and produced a tune that sounded like it was straight out of an old noir film. "This one was written long after I died," he said, still playing. "*Blue in Green*. Sounds better with a whole band—trumpet, sax, drums, bass —but it's good like this too."

Flip pictured Humphrey Bogart nursing a cigarette and whiskey in a bar. Maybe he was trying to crack a case, or maybe he was brooding over the femme fatale. Either way, *Blue in Green* was in the background. Funny how music could so easily convey a setting and mood, even without lyrics. A musician used notes the way a writer used words.

When the song was over, Scratch seemed to consider for a moment. "I'll play one more and then I'll let you rest. You got a date tomorrow." He punctuated this with a *ta-dah!* cord on the piano before launching into a new song. Flip found this one bluesier and was delighted when Scratch started singing. The lyrics were about somewhere called Beale Street, which sounded like a hoppin' place.

When it was over, Flip clapped again. "You have a good voice."

"Passable. I play better than I sing."

Scratch stood, stretched, and sauntered over. He leaned down and pressed a chaste kiss to Flip's forehead. Then he picked up the umbrella and walked to the door. "Sleep well. Don't wanna be too tired for— what was his name?"

"Tony Bergeron," Flip said through a yawn. And the dream ended.

BY MORNING the storm had blown away the hot, stifling air, leaving a chill that caused Flip to shiver before getting dressed. His dream still unusually sharp in his mind, he decided to go out for food and coffee. He'd already discovered a cute place on Ursuline Street, just a block over. It had tiled walls and very tempting pastry cases, and one table was tucked into a tight window-side niche that was perfect for people-watching.

He bundled his laptop into a case, put on a hoodie as an extra layer, and slipped into his tennis shoes. After opening his apartment door, he saw a piece of folded white paper lying on the mat. *To the guy in Apt 2C*, it said on the outside. That was him. He picked it up and unfolded it, squinting to read the messy cursive.

Dear neighbor,

We don't mind your taste in music, but can you please keep it down after midnight? That piano was loud.

—Apt 1C

CHAPTER

SIX

"The thing is," Flip explained to Miss Amelie, "I was asleep after midnight. And even if I was sleepwalking or something, I don't own anything that makes music except my phone. Even at full volume, it's not noisy enough to bother the neighbors."

She exhaled a stream of smoke and regarded him, narrow-eyed. "You don't need me to tell you what's what, boy. You already know."

He shook his head and hugged himself. Although it was indeed chilly this morning, he felt as if he was *freezing*, in a way that endless layers of clothing wouldn't help. "I'm afraid I'm losing my mind."

"Maybe it's in your suitcase."

Fuck, his suitcase. He'd been so distracted with Tony and Scratch that he hadn't checked on its status since the previous morning. Whatever. Tracking the

AirTag and calling the airline hadn't done him any good so far.

He needed to return to more urgent matters. "It's not just the neighbors hearing him. I looked up the songs this morning and, sure enough, they all exist, and they all sound exactly like he played them. He told me one of them came out the year he died, and the brothels were shut down the previous year. I looked up all of those things and they all track. But I didn't know about any of that until he told me. At least, I don't *think* I did. Oh! And last night I found a busted umbrella and brought it inside, and he took it with him, and now it's not anywhere in my apartment."

He took a few deep breaths and wished very hard that the world would start making sense again.

Miss Amelie simply shrugged, as unruffled as if they'd been discussing the weather. "I heard on the news the other day that they're overrun with rats over at police HQ. The rats are eating the weed in the evidence room and getting high." She croaked a laugh. "This city got rats. And we got ghosts. Can't do much about either. I prefer ghosts, myself. They're cleaner. And yours is a looker. Sweet too. It's sad when they die so young."

"Mine?"

"Sounds like Scratch has taken a shine to you. I ain't surprised. Been a while since we had someone with a Clear Eye, and you ain't bad-looking yourself."

Flip blushed. "We, uh, kissed. A couple of times." He'd left that part out when he told her about his nighttime visitor, though he wasn't about to go into their more R-rated antics. Not that he thought she'd be shocked. It just felt... private.

For the first time since they'd met, Miss Amelie appeared genuinely surprised. "Can you *feel* him?"

"Um, yeah. I mean, except that he's not real and I'm just dreaming him." He kept saying that even though it was feeling less and less true.

"Woo-eee! I can see 'em just fine, I can hear 'em, but I can't touch 'em. And I'm clearer than most." She tapped the center of her forehead. "That's some talent you got, boy."

"But I don't—"

"Must've been real nice for Scratch. He's lonely, poor soul. You know there's different kinds of ghosts? Some of 'em ain't figured out yet that they're dead. In denial, I guess. Some have unfinished business. Some died with such strong emotions—anger, usually—that they stay tied to this place. Scratch ain't none of those. I asked him once why he's stickin' around, and he said it's 'cause he likes the place so much. I say maybe so, maybe not."

Flip was gaping at her. "You've... talked to him?"

"Course!" she said, flapping her hand dismissively. "I'm friendly with my neighbors."

This was too much to process. If Flip thought about it hard enough, he might be able to devise a way to test her, to prove or disprove her claim. He couldn't come up with an option right now, though. "I'm so fucked up," he moaned.

"Why you gotta complain about this? It ain't hurtin' you none. You got a damn fine man keepin' you company, playing music for you. Wish I had the same."

Rubbing his temples, Flip stood. "I have to go get ready. I have a da—uh, appointment soon."

"Uh-huh," she said knowingly. But she called out to him as he started to walk away. "That was real nice of you to give Scratch a present. Don't look so confused, boy. The umbrella?"

"I didn't— It was just a broken one I brought inside. I have no idea why. And I don't see what a ghost would do with a busted umbrella anyway."

"Did it look broken when he held it?"

Flip frowned as he tried to remember. "Um, no. I don't think so." No evidence of busted spokes or torn fabric, at least as far as Flip had seen. Instead, it had been neatly furled.

"People ain't the only things with an afterlife. Some animals can be ghosts too, although it's rare. And objects too, 'specially if they've spent a lot of time close to people and then met a sudden end."

"There are ghost *umbrellas?*" He held up his hand to stop her from answering. "Never mind. Don't answer. I'm past my maximum weirdness level already today."

Her laughter followed him all the way into his building.

ORDINARILY FLIP WOULD HAVE SPENT the next hour fretting over spectral rain gear and the possibility that either he was completely losing it or he'd done some heavy petting with a ghost. Instead he fretted over Tony. Maybe fretted wasn't exactly the right word. *Worried*, in the sense that a dog might worry a chew toy. Flip kept thinking about how smart Tony clearly was, and how interesting, and the way his face had lit up when Flip had asked good questions.

The truth was that Flip hadn't been on a date—or anything like one—in eons. Not since he first started seeing Ethan over two years ago. And even then they'd been introduced by a mutual acquaintance, hooked up a couple of times, and then just sort of... fell into togetherness. Ethan was a college professor, and the two of them would just hang out in cafés, each on his laptop.

Did Flip look stupid in the vintage sweater? The young woman at the shop had told him it looked great on him, but of course she was trying to sell the thing. He really wished he had his second-favorite pair of jeans, but they were in his suitcase, and his suitcase was... not here.

He didn't have butterflies in his stomach; he had fucking Mothra.

Flip arrived at the Bergeron-Catanzaro house a few minutes before two. Tony stood on the front porch, conversing with a short, fiftyish woman with spiky copper hair. He beamed when he saw Flip. "You made it!"

"I wasn't about to miss out on a tour from such a knowledgeable guide." Flip climbed the few steps to join them.

Tony introduced the woman, who was the director of the foundation that ran the house. She shook Flip's hand, told them both to have a good time, and ducked inside.

"That sweater's amazing," said Tony.

Mothra settled down a little. "Thanks. I bought it here. I mean, over there." He pointed in what he thought was the general direction of the shop.

"Good find, and it suits you. If you're into that sort of thing, I can recommend a shop over on Magazine Street. Hell, we can go there today if you want. Make it part of the tour." Tony's cheeks colored slightly and he ducked his head. "Historian," he said in explanation. "I'm a huge nerd for old things."

"I'd enjoy seeing that shop. My luggage is in limbo and I could use a couple more things to wear."

Tony lifted his head. "Excellent."

They began in the blocks surrounding the Bergeron-Catanzaro house. Tony showed Flip the Ursuline convent, the French Market, and Jackson Square. They walked to the river, where Tony talked about the shipping industry and how it had shaped New Orleans—and how hurricanes had shaped it too. He was a fascinating speaker. Full of knowledge, thrilled to answer questions, and pleased to learn that Flip was more interested in the everyday events that had happened than in murders, vodou, or vampires. Flip didn't divulge his very recent ghostly visitations—if that's what they were—which had been more than enough supernatural shit as far as Flip was concerned.

They strolled through Tremé, a neighborhood where free people of color lived in the early nineteenth century. Tony took them to Congo Square, now a part of Armstrong Park, which led to a discussion of music. "It's like our food," Tony explained. "People brought their traditions from Africa and Europe and the Caribbean and mixed 'em together to create something new and wonderful."

"Creole," said Flip, remembering what Tony had told him the other day.

"You're an A-plus student for sure."

They strolled for a while after that. Sometimes Tony pointed out something of interest but they also talked about other things. Flip learned that Tony had grown up in the city, moved to New York to attend college, and had worked for a time at a museum there, helping run educational programs for kids on field trips. But New Orleans had pulled him back, and after he'd attended grad school there, he found his dream job at the house his ancestors had once lived in.

As for Flip, he talked about his books a little bit, but only because Tony seemed genuinely curious about them. "I love the way an author can make a reader travel in space and time," said Tony. "It's magic."

That was nice to hear.

And then Tony paused on a street corner. "This neighborhood might not look very exciting now, but a little over a hundred years ago, it was hopping. The city council decided to locate all the brothels here. Made it easier for the rich folks to control things, keep their fingers in the pots. It became a big tourist attraction. Some of the houses were cribs, just dumps where a man could rent some poor woman for fifty cents. But some were grand mansions where customers could sip cocktails and listen to good music."

Flip froze. "Music?"

"Sure. You could argue that Storyville was the birthplace of jazz."

Of course it was. Flip must have heard about all this a while ago and then forgotten about it. He hadn't learned about Storyville from a ghost in his dream—because, despite Miss Amelie's views, ghosts didn't exist.

He struggled to maintain his composure. "I think I, uh, heard something about the military closing it all down?"

"That's right. There were a lot of soldiers and sailors shipping out of here during World War I, and the brass wasn't happy that their boys were spending free time with our girls. And with some of our boys, for that matter, but that wasn't nearly so open. Anyway, the Secretary of War made them shut it all down. It didn't end prostitution, of course, but I guess it satisfied somebody. It also put a lot of those musicians out of work."

Musicians like Scratch.

SEVEN

"Pregaming dinner was a good idea," said Tony after wiping his mouth with a napkin. "And I'm always up for oysters." He apparently realized his unintended double entendre and, charmingly, blushed.

Laughing felt good. "You don't have to be so kind about it. I was really—"

"You were hungry and tired and probably footsore, and it was time to take a break. I'm glad we did."

Flip had concocted that fiction to explain his response to Tony's revelation. It wasn't an absolute lie because, in fact, Flip hadn't yet eaten that day—the note about the piano had disrupted his brunch plans—and they had walked a good bit by that point. But what had caused him to go pale and weak wasn't a skipped meal; it was learning that everything Scratch had told him about Storyville was true. The implications of that terrified him.

Flip had looked so awful that Tony initially offered to call 911, and then suggested an alternative: calling a taxi to take Flip home. But dammit, Flip had truly been enjoying their time together and didn't want it to end. So he'd suggested a snack instead, and now he'd pulled himself together enough to continue their tour. He'd process the whole Scratch thing later. Preferably in private.

As they ate, Tony asked questions about California, which he'd never visited, and then they'd swapped notes on some of their favorite books. It felt distinctly date-like, although neither of them acknowledged it. And Flip was too emotionally precarious at the moment to ask for clarity. Better just to let things flow.

After Flip had insisted on paying and they walked outside, Tony asked, "Are you sure you're still up for more today? I'm really hoping you say yes buuuut I've been told I can be overly enthusiastic and I don't want to overwhelm you."

Seriously, if Flip looked up *charming* in the dictionary, he'd see this man's picture. "I'm definitely up for it, if I haven't scared you away with my fit of the vapors."

Grinning, Tony fluttered his eyelashes and pressed a palm to his chest. Then he spoke in an exaggerated southern accent. "I declare, Mr. Devin, I do believe you've underestimated me."

This time Flip's near swoon had nothing to do with ghosts. Tony was just so…. God, Flip couldn't remember ever losing his head so quickly over anyone. *Slow down*, he reminded himself. *Proceed with caution.*

They took a streetcar into the Garden District. The car was too crowded for Tony to point out any of the sights they passed, but that was okay because Flip had an excuse to stand very close to him. Close enough that sometimes the ride jostled them together, which Tony didn't seem to mind either.

After disembarking, they walked a few blocks to Magazine Street, lined as far as Flip could see with shops, restaurants, and other businesses. As best as he could tell, the pedestrians seemed a nice mix of locals and tourists, and chain stores and franchises were sparse.

As Tony had promised, he led them into a resale clothing shop with a large selection and scanned the racks with what seemed like a practiced eye. "A few years ago I went through a phase where I wore a lot of vintage clothing. The kind of stuff I saw people wearing in old family photos. I figured it helped get me in the mood to... do history."

"You don't do it anymore?" Flip took in Tony's jeans, blue-and-white paisley button-up shirt, and black leather jacket. He looked amazing, but not especially retro.

"It was an expensive habit. I still have a couple of old suits, though."

The two of them had fun selecting items, modeling them, and critiquing each other's choices. In the end,

Tony got a tweed jacket that Flip privately thought made him look like a hot professor—and not at all like Ethan, thankfully. Flip settled on an old pair of Levi's, a pair of gray pleated trousers that he might never wear but fit him well and made Tony wolf-whistle, and a pale-green polo shirt that Tony said brought out the color of his eyes.

"Will that tide you over until your suitcase arrives?"

"I've given up hope that I'll see it again. But this is fine. I don't need much stuff." That wasn't absolutely true. He still wanted the things he'd lost.

"Ah, a minimalist. I admire that. I collect stuff I don't have room for."

Flip suspected that it was highly interesting stuff. "When I was a kid, I bounced around a lot, so I got used to not accumulating. I do have a bunch of books in storage back in Berkeley, though."

Tony's eyes sparkled. "Want to visit a bookstore?"

"Always."

They took a roundabout route so that Flip could goggle at the beautiful houses and Tony could talk about local architecture and some of the elite families who'd lived in this neighborhood. "A lot of authors have lived around here, or at least spent some time," said Tony.

"Did you have relatives here?"

"Nah. Some of them weren't white enough, and none of them were rich enough. As near as I can tell, my most recent wealthy ancestors died in the mid-nineteenth century. You've already seen their house, though, and it wasn't here." He gave a bright smile.

They ended up at the same bookshop Flip had already visited, but he was happy to go again. As he perused the section that showcased local authors, he heard Tony's triumphant cry, several rows away. A moment later, Tony hurried toward him, holding a book aloft like a prize. "It's yours!" he announced.

Flip hadn't previously checked to see whether the store carried any of his titles, and although he tried to look cool, he was secretly thrilled that Tony had found one. "Oh that's *Ball and Chain.*" Oh so nonchalant.

Tony examined the cover: a stylized depiction of, well, a ball and chain spread atop a bed. "What's it about?"

Long ago, Flip had learned that there was no way to answer the question without making a book sound boring and stupid—or hopelessly confusing. But he did his best. "Um, redemption, I guess. The protagonist ends up in a bad marriage that harms him and his wife. And their kids, when they have them. He does some shitty things. So does she. They're both really angry and hurt. But they gradually grow into better people and try to fix things."

"Is it any good?" Tony asked teasingly.

"My biggest seller." Then Flip admitted with slight awkwardness, "Won an award. Got me a three-book deal."

Tony clutched it to his chest. "I'm buying it. You'll sign it, right?"

"Aw, man, you don't have to—"

"No force on earth could stop me from purchasing this book."

Flip realized that they'd attracted the attention of several nearby shoppers, who now stared curiously. Tony noticed too. "This is Flip Devin. You should buy his books. I haven't read them yet because I've just met him, but spending time with him is fantastic. And not just because he's cute."

As everyone laughed, Flip felt his face heat. The thing about being an author was that—unless you were huge like Stephen King—people rarely recognized you. There were some definite benefits to anonymity. He didn't think he was the type who'd enjoy the attention of paparazzi. But it was also sort of nice to be briefly recognized, even if only by a handful of bookshop customers.

Tony took pity on him and lowered his voice. "Are you going to get a book too?"

"Can you recommend one on New Orleans history?"

"I think I can manage that." Tony spent a few minutes peering at the shelves, his mouth pursed thoughtfully, as if this decision was important. Finally he nodded to himself and pulled out a specific volume. "A lot of these books are great. But you seemed pretty interested in Storyville, so you can start with this one."

Flip took the book. "Does it talk about the musicians?"

"A little, yeah. And also the Black women who ran

the houses—some of them got very rich—and the politicians who stuck their fingers into everything."

What if the book mentioned a pianist named Scratch? Well, that would provide his final confirmation. "I'll buy this one," he announced.

Two other people obeyed Tony's earlier command, each purchasing one of Flip's books and asking him to sign. That left a couple of his books on the shelves—one copy each of two titles—and the salesperson had Flip sign those too. As Tony chatted with the other buyers, Flip inscribed the flyleaf of his book.

"Well, at least I've had some income today," said Flip after he and Tony made their way outside. It had grown dark by then, and the city's wildly uneven sidewalks made walking a little hazardous. They strolled slowly past a cemetery, pausing to peer through the locked gate, and then headed back to Magazine Street.

They paused at one point, Tony standing close. "You've been incredibly patient with my lectures today."

"I love your lectures." That was the absolute truth. Flip felt as if he could listen to Tony for years and never get tired of him.

"Yeah?" Shining eyes and a slightly cocked head.

"Yeah."

For several moments they simply stood and stared at each other. Flip felt slightly fizzy, as if he were a little drunk on champagne, and he had to stuff his hands into his pockets to keep from touching.

Then Tony gave a small sigh. "How about something more substantial than those oysters? What food do you like?"

Flip would have happily consumed a bowl of swamp mud if that kept him in Tony's company. "Take us somewhere you like."

That earned a smile.

They ended up at an unpretentious café with a bright and airy interior and sat at one of the few unoccupied tables. Lively conversations filled the space, and servers rushed around with overflowing plates. A majority of the menu items were breaded and deep-fried, and Flip's stomach grumbled at the delicious smells. "Everything looks amazing. How am I supposed to choose?"

"You can point at random. Nothing here's gonna disappoint." Tony briefly chewed his lip. "Hey, will it make you uncomfortable if I order a beer?"

"You noticed I abstained at the oyster place, huh?"

"Yeah, and you only wanted to peek inside the Carousel Bar. I'm perfectly fine with an iced tea."

So Tony was considerate too. Seriously, the man was too perfect; he had to have a fatal flaw. "I appreciate you asking, but order whatever you like. I'm not really a drinker but it doesn't bother me when other people imbibe." Then, because he felt as if Tony's thoughtfulness deserved an explanation, he added, "My parents were drunks and addicts. I've always figured it's better if I sort of... avoid the first steps on that path."

Tony regarded him closely, and maybe he would

have said something except the waitress arrived. Like Flip, Tony ordered iced tea.

"You really didn't have to do that," said Flip after the waitress left.

"I wanted to. I'd rather be completely sober around you anyway. So I don't miss a thing."

Flip's heart made a funny little bounce, and he realized he was giving a sappy smile. "Yeah?"

"I can't remember when I've had a better day. You're damn good company, Flip."

"I'd say the same about you."

Now they were both grinning at each other, and Flip decided this must be an official date, which made him feel giddy. His life may have taken a hard turn into the bizarre lately, but he really couldn't complain about where he'd landed.

The waitress returned with their drinks, laughed—probably at them making googly eyes across the table—and took their orders. Flip actually did point at random. "Fried chicken's gonna take a little longer to cook," the waitress warned him. "You okay with that, honey?"

"I'm in no hurry." He could sit here with Tony for the rest of the week, as far as he was concerned.

"So," said Tony after a long swallow of tea, "*Ball and Chain*. What inspired you to write it?"

"It's not autobiographical, if you're wondering. I've never been married, I'm not attracted to women, and I don't have any kids. I guess there's a little of my parents in that story, except neither of them made any attempt to fix things."

"No redemption there, huh?"

"Not in this life. My father died years ago. Mom... dunno. Lost touch." He didn't feel a pang over it and doubted she did either.

"Do you want me to stop asking questions about your family?"

"No, it's just...." How to explain this to a guy who'd traced his roots back two hundred years, whose literal life work involved studying aspects of his lineage? "I don't have any other relatives, and it's been a long time since my parents mattered to me. So you can ask, but there's just not much to tell. I'd love to hear more about your folks, though."

So Tony told him about his mother and father and siblings—he had three—and aunts and uncles and cousins. Flip would need a spreadsheet to keep track of it all, but that was fine. Tony did a beautiful job of making all of these people seem complex and interesting, as if they were characters in a really great book.

The food, when it eventually arrived, proved to be as wonderful as promised. Possibly the best fried chicken Flip had ever tasted, and the sides were good too: mac and cheese, green beans, and cornbread. But his companion remained the star of the show, handsome and funny and fascinating.

"Why New Orleans?" asked Tony, chasing red beans and rice with his spoon.

Why indeed. "Abbreviated version. I've wanted to be a writer since... forever. Got a degree in English, which meant I ended up with a string of jobs that barely paid the bills. I was working at a hotel in Napa when I met Ethan, a college prof who was up there for the weekend. Then a lot of things happened kinda fast: got an agent, sold a book, quit my job, moved in with Ethan in the Bay Area. Sold a couple more books. Then my writing slowed down, Ethan cheated, I packed up my shit, and I decided to give myself a writing residency here until my savings run out."

Tony didn't run away screaming, which was impressive. "Cheated."

"He's a bastard, but we weren't good together anyway." Fuck. He might as well hit Tony with the truth. "I'm not sure I'm good with anyone."

"We've been pretty good today."

"It's been one day. I'd fuck things up eventually."

Troy pointed his spoon at Flip. "This is presumptuous of me since we've just met. But in case you haven't noticed, I'm not exactly known for keeping my mouth shut. My family's nickname for me is Yak-Yak, and I sort of can't believe I just admitted that, but there you go."

"I like it," said Flip, smiling despite the general seriousness of the conversation.

"There's a lot of eccentricity in my family tree, in case you hadn't noticed that either. We don't always embrace one another's weirdnesses, but at least we tolerate them. When my sister Nicole was eighteen and decided she was a vampire—too much Anne Rice or something, I don't know—we humored her, even though it meant she refused to leave her room unless it was dark outside. When my cousin— Well, you get the idea."

"She didn't exsanguinate people, did she?"

Chuckling, Tony shook his head. "No, she just insisted on eating her meat really rare. She outgrew that phase. Nowadays she's vegan. Anyway, my great-aunt Amelie claims to be a psychic, and—" He stopped because Flip was choking on a mouthful of green beans.

"Miss Amelie?" he managed when he could breathe again. "The one with the table on St. Philip Street?"

Tony looked pleased. "You know her?"

"Uh, yeah. I live across the street."

He should tell Tony the whole tale, including the parts about Scratch. But he really, really didn't want to.

For the moment, at least, Tony seemed more intrigued than anything. "Huh. Did she...? Well, let me explain why I brought her up to you. You know, she's not even a Bergeron. She married into us, and either she was woo-woo before or the eccentricity is contagious. A few months ago, at Christmas dinner, I was kind of whining about not being able to find the right man to settle down with. *She* said that's because there's a particular someone I'm supposed to be with but he hasn't arrived yet." He said the next words in a passable imitation of her scratchy voice. *"He's gonna think he's lost everything, but he ain't. Boy just needs to make enough room for you. You two got stories to tell."*

"And you think she meant me? She wasn't that specific."

Tony just looked at him, eyebrows raised, until Flip conceded with a nod. "Okay, sounds like me," he said. "But surely Miss Amelie isn't omniscient. And fated mates? That's a romance trope, not real life."

"She meant fitted, not fated." Tony illustrated this by interlocking his two index fingers. Then he ducked his head. "This is far too much to lay on a man who's just met me. I'm sorry."

Flip didn't feel as if they'd just met. He'd been so comfortable with Tony that he'd let down his guard in a way he rarely did, even after weeks or months of knowing someone. He believed what Tony was telling him and, more than that, *wanted* to believe what Miss Amelie had predicted. Sharing stories with Tony Bergeron seemed like the most delightful future imaginable.

But almost everything that had happened since his arrival in New Orleans had been bizarrely surreal, and Tony—a really good person—didn't deserve to be dragged into a swamp of weirdness.

"I've scared you off," Tony said sadly.

"No. But... it's complicated."

That brought a deep sigh. "It always is."

The waitress came by and was disappointed to see them drooping rather than flirting. She was even more disappointed when they said they'd pass on dessert. "You're gonna want our bread pudding with rum sauce to go then, honey. If you don't, you'll be sad about it."

They already had enough sadness, so Flip gave in and ordered one for each of them.

Although they rode the streetcar back to the Quarter together, they didn't say much. Tony looked unhappy, which made Flip feel bad, but he just couldn't bring himself to talk about Miss Amelie's predictions or about Scratch. He was too confused about it himself. And maybe it was just as well. Tony deserved someone a lot better than him—steadier, nicer, more connected. It was kinder to separate from him now, before things went any further. As it was, even the idea of not seeing Tony again made Flip ache.

"I don't even know where you live," said Flip as they began the trek toward St. Philip. "Is this out of your way?"

"I've got a place on Clouet Street in the Bywater. I'd pass by your apartment anyway. But if you want I can take a different route."

He sounded forlorn, which broke Flip's heart. "I'd like to walk with you."

Tony rewarded him with a small smile.

Although Flip would have preferred to be unencumbered—they both carried various bags with clothing, books, and dessert—at least they didn't have very far to go. Maybe a mile or so. And there was no point in remaining silent, so Flip asked some questions about things they passed, and Tony brightened as he got to explain.

Flip was genuinely sorry when they got to St. Philip.

"Ah," said Tony, pointing. "Aunt Amelie's usual spot." She had packed up for the night, of course, and the street was deserted. "Look, don't be scared by what she said. She doesn't mean any harm by it."

"I believe that."

Tony scuffed his toe on the pavement. "I think that there are some places where the line between everyday and the uncanny has worn thin. The city of New Orleans is one of them. I dunno why—maybe it's the river's fault. Things that would be impossible in most places are possible here. Like old ladies who can see the future."

And ghosts, Flip thought. He nodded. "If I stayed here long enough, maybe I'd get used to it. But I'm only here for a few months."

Tony frowned, scuffed his toe again, and then squared his shoulders. "Well, if you decide you want more tour guidance, I'd like that. You know where to find me." He pointed toward the Bergeron House.

"Thanks for that. And thanks for... everything." Flip's throat felt tight. He wanted to grab Tony's hand, drag him up to his apartment and its enormous bed, and stay there together indefinitely.

"It was, quite literally, my pleasure."

Flip didn't move to open the door to his building, and Tony didn't walk away. They stood there, a tableau under the flickering gaslight. Were there ghosts watching them? Flip couldn't tell.

Finally Tony cleared his throat. "I'm going to go

home and read your book. I hope you like the one I picked out for you."

"Maybe it'll give me some ideas for my next novel."

"I like that," said Tony thoughtfully. "We hear things about the big players, but there are so many others who are forgotten. I think that's partly why I chose my career—to preserve their stories. Some of those people were my family, after all. The ones who owned the Bergeron House, the ones who were born enslaved but managed to buy their freedom, the ones who sold rice calas in the Quarter, the ones who played the piano in whorehouses."

Flip felt as if someone had suddenly filled his spine with ice water. "Piano?" he croaked.

"Yeah. I had a great-great-great uncle who, according to family lore, was a pretty good player. In both senses of the word, actually. He apparently spent his free time hopping into bed with anyone—male or female—who'd have him. Which eventually got him murdered."

Really, Flip didn't have to ask. But he did anyway, barely able to hear his own voice over the rushing in his ears. "What was his name?"

Tony grinned. "Anthony—same as me. But he had a nickname. He performed as Scratch Bergeron."

CHAPTER

EIGHT

At least this time Flip didn't almost faint. Maybe it was because, deep in his heart, he'd known the truth all along. But knowing something and accepting it were two different things, and Flip had finally hit the limits of his denial.

Ghosts and clairvoyants existed. Flip himself possessed a talent for interacting with the departed. He'd even made out with one of them. And that ghost he'd entertained in his bed was also Tony's relative.

Now that he accepted this reality, what was he supposed to do with it?

"Is Scratch in the book I bought?" He was proud of how calm he sounded.

"No. Nobody knows about him except a few of my octogenarian family members, and who knows how accurate their stories are. None of them were born yet when he died." Tony gave a wry chuckle. "I don't think there's a single person alive now who knew him."

You're wrong about that, Flip thought.

But Tony was still speaking. "I've dug around and found a few mentions of him. There used to be these books, the Blue Books, that were guides to the Storyville brothels. There were advertisements in there too, for all sorts of things. I've seen his name mentioned in a couple of the ads. I also found a newspaper article about his murder. But that's about it."

"Do you have a photo of him?"

Tony looked puzzled. "No. Why?"

Flip fumbled for a reasonable response, but then Tony answered his own question. "Oh. I bet you're a visual processor. Is that a writer thing?"

"I have no idea," Flip answered honestly.

After a moment of slightly awkward silence, Tony shifted the bag in his hand. "Well, I have to work in the morning, and you probably have to...." His voiced trailed away and he sighed deeply. "Thanks for a really great day, Flip."

"It was my pleasure too."

After a bit more bittersweet discomfiture, they parted.

The first thing Flip did after depositing his new clothing and book in the bedroom was to heat the bread pudding according to the waitress's instructions. Then, even though he wasn't hungry, he ate it. The sweet stickiness comforted him and calmed his uneasy stomach. Fortified, he booted up his laptop and pounded out two new chapters. He followed up with an email to his long-suffering agent, in which he informed her that, contrary to fears, he had a good chance of completing the manuscript by the end of the month. She'd be thrilled to wake up to that news.

It was very late by then, so Flip went to bed.

His dream began with standing alone at the French window and looking outside. He saw nobody, living or dead. Hearing a small sound, he turned to discover Scratch at the other end of the room, wearing a tuxedo but looking uncharacteristically subdued.

"You still have the umbrella," said Flip, even though they both knew it was irrelevant.

Scratch bounced the furled umbrella against his forearm. "It's nice. Do you want it back?"

"Keep it. Um, do ghosts need umbrellas?"

"Not to keep dry. But this one here reminds me of when I was alive. Carrying it makes me feel more substantial." He jutted out his chin a bit, as if making a point.

Flip said, "I know you're real."

"Been telling you that."

"Now I believe you."

"Did *he* convince you that ghosts exist? Tony Bergeron?"

Flip shook his head. "I didn't tell him about you. But he was telling me about his family and mentioned you."

Clearly surprised, Scratch blinked rapidly. "He knows about me?"

"A little, yeah. He says he's researched you but couldn't find many details."

"Researched?" Looking a little dazed, Scratch crossed the room and sat on a straight-backed chair that didn't exist when Flip was awake. "He researched *me?*"

"He heard a few family stories about you and tried to look you up in old records. There were some ads with your name and, uh, a newspaper article about...." Not wanting to mention the murder, Flip made a vague hand gesture instead.

But Scratch had conjured a tentative, sweet smile. "They remember me? You ain't tryin' to fool me, are you?"

Great. This made him the second Bergeron today to break Flip's heart. "I'm not fooling you. They do remember."

"I ain't never met him. Ain't seen none of my family since I died." He spread his hands. "I can't go far from here, and none of 'em have come close enough for me to see. Sometimes I hear a little from other ghosts. Our... territories overlap a little, yeah? So we can pass news on. But facts get lost or changed...."

Like a spectral game of telephone. "What about Miss Amelie?" Flip asked.

"Ah, my *jolie fille*. She tells me things too, when she can. But she ain't like you—she can only see me every now and then, and not for long."

"Okay, but couldn't she tell your other relatives about you? Then they could come visit you."

Scratch shrugged. "She tried a few times over the years. Got tired of 'em tellin' her she's crazy."

Well, Flip could understand that. He'd doubted her even after seeing Scratch himself. "It must be frustrating for you."

"Something like that." Scratch chewed his lip for a moment, staring down at the floor. Then he looked up. "It hurts. Not a physical pain—I'm past all that. But a pain nonetheless. I lost my future, my connections. I'm not a *part* of anything no more. Can't do nothing that makes a difference. Can't even sit and have a cold drink and shoot the breeze with someone, feeling the sweat trickle down my back and smelling good food on the stove. Can't go down to the river and watch the boats. Can't... can't touch nobody. Until you."

He stood and walked to Flip, grasped Flip's shoulders almost too hard, and kissed him.

There was fire in this kiss, and desperate need— and not all of it was from Scratch. Even with his eyes closed, Flip could picture the two of them, lit up like a Bourbon Street sign, crackling with energy like a thunderstorm. The kiss flooded him and he welcomed it, wanted to submerge himself in it. Didn't even care if it destroyed him.

But then he staggered back, out of Scratch's grip. "Tony," he rasped.

"Nobody calls— Oh." Scratch's jaw tightened. "Him."

"I spent the day with him."

"So? I'm here and he's not. He's got no claim on you."

Technically, that was true. They'd just met and hadn't so much as kissed. Neither had made the other any promises, and when Tony had reached out for something more, Flip had clearly turned away. And sure, there was Miss Amelie's prediction, but even if it wasn't complete bullshit, it didn't obligate Flip in any way. He hadn't consented to being a party to whatever she had in mind for him and Tony. Hell, neither had Tony.

Yet Flip felt that if he were to follow through with Scratch, they'd both be betraying Tony.

"I can't," he said with genuine regret.

"He's *alive*. He's got the whole world. I got a couple blocks in the Quarter and you."

"You don't have me. Neither does Tony. Fuck, I barely have myself. I feel like I've been falling apart, bit by bit, for years, and now I don't even have the ground beneath me anymore. I can't... I just *can't*, Scratch."

Scratch's shoulders sagged and he swallowed a few times. "It's not fair of me to ask. You didn't choose any of this."

"Neither did you."

"I made bad decisions, and—"

"And so did I, and here we are. But I think this"—Flip waved a hand between them—"would be a bad decision too."

After a pause, Scratch nodded. He bent and picked up the umbrella from the floor next to the straight-backed chair. "Thanks for this," he said, holding it up, "and for your company. They've both meant a lot to me."

Then he was gone, and Flip was alone in his dream.

82

CHAPTER

NINE

Flip woke up feeling tired, as if he hadn't slept at all. He felt a double sense of loss—Tony and Scratch—even though he'd never had either of them. Even though he'd only recently met them and one of them was long dead.

Still, words were pushing at his brain, so he brewed coffee, sat at his laptop, and wrote. Wrote a lot, in fact, so that he could almost see the end of the manuscript, the way the first light of dawn peeked over the horizon before the sun truly rose. The entire time he worked, he felt as if he were seeing the events of the story unfold in front of him; all he needed to do was attempt to record them coherently. A Clear Eye might help someone picture scenes, but the words themselves had to be found, and that was still hard work. Hard, but satisfying.

When his stomach loudly insisted that caffeine alone did not a meal make, he saved the file, backed it up, and checked his email. His agent had replied and, judging from the number of exclamation points, was thrilled that he was finally making progress. It was good to have one person on the planet who he wasn't currently disappointing.

There was also a message from the airline, assuring him that his luggage piece was on the way to New Orleans. He didn't bother to track the AirTag to confirm.

Although he had some food in the house, he decided it would be a good idea to get out and walk around a little before diving back into work. After a quick shower, he got dressed. Spying the book he'd bought the previous day, he grabbed it before walking out the door. It might be nice to do some reading over lunch.

Miss Amelie was in her usual spot, but she had customers: a middle-aged white couple wearing matching American flag T-shirts. She waved at him, and Flip sent her a series of hand gestures that was supposed to mean *You and I will talk later.*

At his favorite café—he had one of those now, it seemed—he settled in with a sandwich, more coffee, and the book, which turned out to be really interesting. There was no mention of Scratch specifically, but the author discussed bordello musicians in general. The writing was informative but also engaging enough to make him feel as if he were there, sitting in a whorehouse in Storyville over a hundred years ago. Ever since he was very young, he'd possessed an almost uncanny ability to sink into the world of the books he read. That was likely how he'd been able to survive his miserable childhood; whatever was going on around him, he had an escape. Now he wondered if he had his Clear Eye to thank for that skill.

When he realized that the café was getting ready to close, Flip headed outside and into the sunny, temperate weather. He strolled aimlessly for a time—well, not entirely aimlessly, in that he took care to avoid passing too close to the Bergeron-Catanzaro house.

Eventually he turned onto St. Philip. Miss Amelie gestured him over, as if he needed any urging. He threw himself into the empty chair with more dramatic flair than he usually displayed.

"That's a good book," she said, pointing.

"Tony recommended it."

"That boy is something, ain't he? Cute as a button and smart as a whip."

He scowled at her. "I don't need a matchmaker."

She widened her eyes in a completely unconvincing charade of innocence.

"Look, Miss Amelie. I'm a mess. I was a mess even before I started believing in psychic powers and ghosts, and—"

"Ah, so now you accept the obvious."

Flip crossed his arms. "Ghosts are not obvious."

"They are to you. It's funny that you'd rather doubt your own sanity than believe in spirits, even when that spirit is a good one." She waggled her finger at him.

"They're not all like Scratch, boy. Consider yourself lucky."

"I don't— It doesn't— Stop trying to redirect the conversation. You told Tony that he and I are fated mates."

"I did no such thing." When Flip raised his eyebrows, she laughed. "I only told him you were coming, is all. Ain't nothing wrong with that."

"You said—or you strongly implied—that we were meant to be together."

"That's just stating a fact, now. All people are connected like beads on a string. Some far apart, some real close. You two are next to each other, and if you look, you'll see that for yourself. Tony *can't* see it, though, and all I did was tell him 'cause he was feelin' down."

She made it all sound so reasonable.

"Look, Miss Amelie. You're acting like it's simple, but it's not. Tony is—well, he's pretty much amazing, actually—but I'm a mess. He needs someone like him, someone who has his life together. That's not me. And God, there's Scratch, and I'm almost broke, and I'm only here for a few months, and...." Flip flung his arms wide and made a sound intended to convey the hopelessness of the situation.

Miss Amelie was clearly not impressed. "Since when is life supposed to be easy, boy? It is what it is. You make the most of it or you don't. That's your choice. But you can't change facts."

As if facts were something solid you could hang on

to. He was an author—he knew that truth was subjective and reality was what you made of it. And sometimes the whole universe could twist on you overnight. While you dreamed.

"So what am I supposed to do?" He heard the plea in his voice.

She shook her head. "Ain't my job to tell you. I'm like a good pair of glasses—I help people see more clearly. Glasses don't tell you what to do with what you see. And you don't need glasses, boy. You see just fine on your own when you open your Eye."

This was supremely unhelpful and also not at all comforting. He waited while a flower-bedecked mule slowly pulled a cart of tourists past. He sort of envied the animal. Sure, it had a heavy burden to bear, but at least it didn't have to agonize about what direction to take. It had someone to care for it and make sure it didn't wander off somewhere it shouldn't.

"I make shitty decisions," he finally announced. "I moved in with someone I shouldn't have. Ditched the day job because I thought I could make it as an author. Wrote a couple good books and then stalled right after signing a deal. Fled California to a city I barely know. Picked an apartment just because the street and I share a name. Spent the day with a man who's too good for me. And those are just the latest hits."

"Huh." Miss Amelie leaned back in her chair and scrunched up her lips. "Seems to me that if nobody's in prison or dead, those ain't so bad. Sometimes you gotta ride over a lotta potholes to get somewhere good."

That was more of a maxim than good advice, but Flip acknowledged it was all he was going to get. He stood and looked down at her. "I'll see you around, Miss Amelie."

She cackled. "You sure will. Oh, and boy? Sometimes it's a whole lot easier to make a journey if you ain't dragging all your baggage with you."

"My baggage is gone."

"Not yet it ain't."

FLIP WROTE LONG into the night, until he could no longer see the words before him. If he had any dreams, he didn't remember them. He wrote the next day too, and went for a walk, and did some laundry, and bought a few groceries. He waved at Miss Amelie every time he saw her but didn't stop for a chat; she was busy most of the day anyway. Scratch didn't come to him that night. Or the night after, or the night after that. Flip even caught himself consciously widening his Clear Eye, and although he did catch glimpses of a few spectral figures, none of them were Scratch.

A raw sense of loss tore at Flip's gut—for both of the Bergerons he'd met and, apparently, lost.

But the writing... ah. The writing flowed like the Mississippi River, powerful and unstoppable. There had been times in the past when words came easily to him, but they were nothing compared to the present. As soon as he sat at his keyboard, entire scenes opened as easily as unfolding a kitchen towel, and when he wasn't in front of his computer, the characters clamored eagerly to be set free again.

Less than two weeks after he'd arrived in New Orleans, his book had grown from thirty thousand to nearly a hundred thousand words, and two days after that, he typed The End. Then he backed up the completed manuscript, walked to a dive bar on Royal Street, and got incredibly drunk.

Well, he tried to anyway. It was a ritual for him, and one of the few exceptions to his usual abstinence: when a first draft was completed, he celebrated with booze. He couldn't remember why he'd started this tradition, but once he had, it seemed unlucky to change it. So tonight he rapidly downed four Sazeracs —the specific cocktail chosen in honor of his current city—which should have been more than enough to put him under the table. He waited for the fuzziness to descend. He'd always loved that fuzziness, which was another reason why he almost never allowed himself to drink. It would be all too easy to slip into that state permanently. Tonight, however, his head remained stubbornly clear. He ordered a fifth and then a sixth drink, more than he'd ever consumed at once and enough to make the lanky bartender stare at him with concern.

But he stayed sober.

Swearing under his breath, he slid off the bar stool

and walked out into the night. The air was warm and still, making him think about mosquitoes and yellow fever, although as far as he could tell, nothing actually bit him. His feet led him out of the Quarter to Frenchmen Street, where music streamed out of open doors, but he didn't enter any of the buildings. He stood on a street corner, imagining a handsome man playing a piano.

All the way home he saw ghosts, but none were familiar. They weren't frightening, just ordinary people going about their business despite being dead. A spectral mother and child sat on a front porch peacefully shelling peas; the child smiled and waved at Flip as he passed, and he waved back. An old man leaned against a wall and drank from a brown glass bottle, swaying slightly to a tune that Flip couldn't hear. A young man walked by with a heavy-looking bag settled on one shoulder. Flip strolled among the ghosts and the living, feeling as if he didn't entirely fit with either category.

He was nearly back to St. Philip Street when he recognized the emotion that clung to all of the ghosts: melancholy. None of them were truly despairing, at least as far as he could tell, but sadness hung on all of them like a shawl. That made sense, he supposed, given that they were dead.

But Flip was alive, so why did he share this emotion as well? He'd finished the manuscript and had the gut sense that he'd written a damn good book. He had a nice place to stay for now and all the basic things he needed to survive. Nobody was trying to murder him for sleeping with the wrong person.

A realization floated just out of reach. He knew it was there, but he couldn't grasp it, which was so fucking frustrating that he nearly walked into another bar. Surely a couple more drinks would finally get him wasted.

Instead he turned onto St. Philip, glanced at the empty spot that Miss Amelie would occupy in the morning, and keyed in the code to enter his building.

His suitcase waited at the foot of the stairs.

CHAPTER

TEN

Flip carried the suitcase into his apartment and left it, unopened, in the living room. He puttered around the kitchen, preparing a favorite comfort food: pasta, creamy with shredded asiago and gruyere. Although the boxed stuff had been a mainstay during his youth, it was pleasant to now stand on his gallery and gaze at quiet streets while spooning the adult version into his mouth.

When he fell asleep soon afterward, his dreams were wispy, insubstantial things that melted away immediately.

He hadn't gone to bed especially late, but he slept until nearly noon and woke up groggy. No headache or other hangover symptoms, however, and his head cleared after he brewed some coffee and reheated the leftover mac and cheese.

Usually he let the first drafts of his writing sit for a while, like seeds tucked into damp soil. That allowed him a fresher eye when he revised them. He could have waited with this one too, since his agent wasn't expecting it for a couple of weeks, but an inexplicable sense of urgency gnawed at him. He sat down at his laptop and dove directly into the second draft. He was delighted—but not surprised—to discover that the manuscript didn't really need much tinkering.

"This is really *good*," he kept saying, because there was no reason to be falsely modest if ghosts were his only audience. As was often the case once a book was finished, he had a sense of distance from it, as if it had been written by someone else. Maybe that didn't make him entirely objective about it, but in this case he was certain that his perception of quality wasn't skewed.

He stayed up all night reading over the manuscript, fixing typos and tweaking a few minor details, mainlining coffee but barely eating. Dawn had already broken by the time he finished. His muscles were cramped, his eyes gritty, his belly hollow. But it was all worth it for the supreme satisfaction he experienced when he wrote a quick email to his agent, attached the document, and hit *Send*.

After which he immediately stumbled off to the bedroom and climbed onto the mattress, still fully clothed.

When Flip opened his eyes again, it was nearly five p.m. and his stomach was staging a protest over being ignored. A nice dinner out felt justified, so he showered, dressed, and ventured out of his apartment.

Miss Amelie was just packing up for the day. She

glanced up from the cart she used to transport her setup. "Congratulations, boy. Told you that all you had to do was open your Eye."

"It's wide open." He paused a moment. "But, um, I haven't seen Scratch for a long time."

"Maybe he don't want to see you. Or maybe your Eye ain't as open as you think."

And maybe the separation was just as well, for Scratch's sake as well as Flip's, but it didn't feel that way. Neither did his self-enforced avoidance of Tony, which Miss Amelie didn't mention.

"I owe my publisher one more book under my contract. Do you envision me writing it in a timely matter?"

"You're already writing it, boy."

She was way off track on that. He didn't have even the germ of an idea for the next one. However, it was too early to start worrying about that, so he wished Miss Amelie a good evening and continued on.

A couple of hours later he returned to his apartment with his belly full. He'd seen ghosts all evening, including a sad-eyed man bussing invisible dishes at the restaurant, and it had been a little difficult to pretend they weren't there. Some of them acknowledged him with polite nods or waves, as if he were an acquaintance, but he was afraid to respond because the living people around him would think he was crazy. He hoped the ghosts understood and didn't assume he was intentionally rude.

It was a bit of a relief to return to the solitude of his place—but also a little bit lonely.

An email from his agent was waiting. In recent months, he'd felt dread and shame every time her name appeared in his inbox, but not today. Especially when he saw the subject line: *Holy shit.*

He grinned while reading the short message.

I was just going to glance at the first few paragraphs, but then I couldn't stop and now I'm most of the way through, my wife and my dog hate me, and I'm so excited I might cry. Home run this time, Flip. Worth every minute of anxious waiting.

Yeah, Flip knew it was good, but it was nice to get some external validation.

Of course, his work wasn't nearly done. There would be several rounds of edits, and although he adored his editor, that was always a grueling process. After that would come all the marketing and promotional stuff that he generally hated, and then the fraught dilemma about whether to read reviews or pretend they didn't exist. And the deadline for the next book felt as if it was looming already.

But all of that could wait.

What he really wished he could do right now was sit with a couple of friends—or a lover—and celebrate his achievement. Nothing flashy. Just a comfortable spot with chill vibes, some tasty snacks and nonalcoholic drinks, and amiable conversation. But Flip had burned most of his friendship bridges long ago, and Ethan had claimed the last of them.

If the Bergeron-Catanzaro house had been open at this hour, Flip probably would have marched over to see Tony. Which would be selfish of him, really; he was the one who'd pushed Tony away. So maybe it was a good thing the place was closed.

Feeling restless, Flip paced his apartment until his gaze fell on the suitcase, still sitting where he'd left it. He dragged it into the bedroom, but after spending a few moments trying to decide whether to open it on the floor or on the bed, he abruptly chose not to open it at all. He'd go for a walk instead.

He wandered for miles, paying little attention to where he went. In Congo Square, ghostly men and women played instruments and danced. Some were dressed in rags, some in finer clothing from more recent eras. Near the Ninth Ward, ghosts waded blank-eyed through invisible flood waters. Near enormous oak trees in City Park, spectral children splashed at the edges of a lake. Near a tangle of freeways and among a crowd of medical and university buildings, a vast empty building loomed, and ghosts stared mournfully at him through glassless windows.

God, why didn't these spirits move on? Why hadn't Scratch? Whatever awaited them beyond this plane, it had to be better than trudging meaninglessly around, unnoticed by almost everyone, untouched and unconnected.

Footsore, Flip was almost home when the answer came to him.

He'd been passing through Jackson Square in front

of the cathedral. The fortunetellers, buskers, and artists had long since gone home, the tourists were back in their hotels, and the cathedral itself, shrouded in fog, looked transported straight out of a gothic novel. But a ghost sat on one of the benches. He was an old man with long gray hair, and his shapeless layers of clothing could have come from any decade in the last century. He clutched a can in one hand.

"Good evening," said Flip since there was nobody near enough to notice.

The ghost raised his can in a salute. "Evenin'."

"It's a good night for a stroll. Not too hot or too cold. Not raining."

"A good night for sittin' too."

Flip paused in front of him. "It's a good place to sit."

"My daughter was baptized in there." The ghost gestured at the cathedral. "She always said she'd be married there too. But she got sick...." His shoulders slumped.

How could you comfort a man who held so tightly to grief that it survived even his own death?

And that was when understanding struck Flip so hard that for a moment he thought there had been an earthquake. He staggered slightly, blinking to clear the literal flash of insight from his eyes. But no, dammit. It was his Eye that needed clearing.

Flip braced himself and opened it wider than he'd imagined possible.

He saw the ghost on the bench, yes, and several

others besides. But he also saw a pair of policemen watching him warily from a block away, and he knew that one of the cops was in the middle of a nasty divorce but would soon meet the love of his life and remarry, and the other cop was worried about an ache he'd been feeling lately in his left knee, which he was soon going to discover was bursitis. An Uber driver a block away was on her way home, looking forward to the leftovers in her fridge and bingeing a sci-fi series on Netflix. A woman staying in an Airbnb a block off the square was pregnant, and although she didn't know it yet, she was going to be overjoyed when she found out. The baby—

No, this was too much. Flip narrowed his vision to the things that were his business.

He saw that the ghost on the bench hadn't moved on because he clung so tightly to his grief. In fact, the reason why *all* ghosts remained was that they were unable to let go of something that tied them to life. There wasn't room in those individuals for the future because the past took up too much space.

Losing things could be terrible—but it could also lead to change. To better things.

What had Miss Amelie said to Tony? *He's gonna think he lost everything, but he ain't. Boy just needs to make enough room for you.*

In a way, Flip was a ghost as well, clutching at lost opportunities, bad decisions, hurtful betrayals, deep-seated fears.

Right then and there, Flip let go of it all, including

his skepticism and self-doubt. All fell away from him like plaster peeling off a façade, and for the first time since he was a young child, he felt as if he could fully expand his lungs.

Hot tears ran down his cheeks, but they were due to relief and joy rather than sorrow. Although he'd already walked for miles, he could have run all night. He could almost have fucking *flown*. A sense of promise filled him. A sense of potential. He was alive, he'd written a damned good book, and he could shape his future however he wished.

Then Flip remembered the rest of what Miss Amelie had said—*You two got stories to tell*—and he knew precisely what he wanted that future to look like.

Although Flip wanted to shout his exultation, he didn't particularly want to have a conversation with those cops; he had better ways to spend his time. So he turned back to the ghost on the bench and smiled. "I have to go right now, but if you like, I can come back another night. I'd love to hear about your daughter if you want to tell me about her."

When the ghost smiled like that, he was almost beautiful. "Really?"

"I want to know about her. I bet she was special."

"She was. She truly was."

Maybe talking about her would free this ghost from enough grief that he'd be able to move on. But even if not, it would surely bring some happiness to his gray existence, and Flip could spare the time.

But right now he had more personal matters to

attend to. He said good-night to the ghost, waved cheerily at the confused cops, and hurried home.

ELEVEN

Now that he'd received his epiphany, Flip had expected Scratch to reappear. But he didn't, not even when Flip wandered around his apartment, Eye wide, calling him. That was disappointing but not devastating. Perhaps Flip could find a way to draw him forward later.

The rest of Flip's plan would have to wait for morning, but he did draft an email to his agent, thanking her for her enthusiasm over the completed manuscript and briefly outlining his idea for the next book. Seeing the proposal actually written out made it seem much more real. He felt exhilarated and a tiny bit terrified, which he thought was a fine combination. A good author shouldn't feel overly comfortable with his or her project; for the manuscript to truly shine, creating it should prove at least moderately challenging.

Even though it was late, he couldn't help but do a bit of background research for the new book and scribble some notes in the battered notebook he dragged around for that purpose.

His dreams didn't include any ghosts that night but they were interesting nonetheless. Mostly they were about forgiveness. Flip forgave Ethan and his parents, not because they necessarily deserved it, but because doing so would be healthiest for him. He forgave himself too, which was harder. Dream-Flip said, "Hominem te memento. Remember you're only human, and sometimes humans screw up."

He felt refreshed as soon as he awoke. He knew he'd fuck up again—and that he'd inevitably be fucked over by others—but he also knew that when these things happened, he possessed the strength to move on. Because if you didn't move on, you were nothing but a ghost.

His agent, an hour ahead of him in New York, had already replied. She seemed enthusiastic about the new book idea. Maybe she was simply relieved that he even had an idea, but that was fine.

A little before nine, Flip grabbed his suitcase, carried it downstairs, and took it outside. Miss Amelie had just arrived in her spot, so he helped her set up. "You leavin' town, boy?" she asked, waving at his suitcase, but her expression said she knew better. She sat in her folding chair and gave him an expectant look.

"I'm sticking around for a while. Do you know anyone who could use some clothing in my size? Nothing fancy, but there's some comfy jeans in there and my favorite old Ramones shirt."

"You don't need any of it?"

Flip shook his head. "I'm making room for something better."

"Uh-huh." She leaned back, looking completely smug. "I know someone. Leave it here."

"Thanks."

"What you gonna do now?"

"Have some breakfast and then, I hope, meet up with a friend. You wanna tell me how that's gonna go?"

She flashed a broad smile. "That's all up to you, boy."

He lingered over breakfast. Partly because the café he'd chosen on Royal Street was nice, with friendly waitstaff and interesting décor. But partly he dawdled because he was nervous about what he had to do next. It could end up in disaster. One thing he was sure about, however, was that attempting it was not a mistake. In this case, backing away fearfully was the bad decision, even if it would be the easiest thing to do.

It was past ten-thirty by the time he paid, girded his mental loins, and headed northeast.

His trek was only a few blocks long, and he'd made it many times before. This morning he noticed how comfortable the walk felt. The scenery was so familiar that it was starting to feel like home.

When he entered the Bergeron-Catanzaro House, a familiar young woman greeted him, and Flip remembered her name: Kat. She clearly recognized him as well. "Back for another tour?" she asked sunnily. "The next one is in about fifteen minutes."

"Actually, I came to see Tony Bergeron. Is he available?"

She displayed neither surprise nor disapproval. "Hang on. I'll text him. Can I tell him your name?"

"Flip."

That did cause her to blink, but he was used to that, and she recovered quickly. She poked at her phone for a moment and then gave him a professional smile. "It may take him a while. He gets buried in projects sometimes and has a hard time detaching. Feel free to look around while you wait. There's a new quilt exhibit in the dining room. It's really cool."

Flip dithered about whether to go look. He believed her that it was a good exhibit, but he was too nervous right now to get anything out of it. Maybe it would be better if—

Tony darted through a doorway at the far end of the hallway and dashed toward him. "Flip!" He tried to slow when he realized that Kat was watching, but it was too late. Her eyebrows shot up, and he blushed but didn't turn away. "Are you here to yell at me about Aunt Amelie?"

"The opposite, actually. Um...." Flip glanced at Kat, unsure how much he should say with an audience.

Tony took the hint. "Sorry, Kat. I'm taking a break." He winked at her, grabbed Flip's hand, and towed him down the hall and out onto the back porch overlooking the courtyard. There was nobody else in sight.

But then Flip, the author, found himself at a loss

for words. He had no clue where to begin. So it was Tony who spoke first. "You came back."

Well, hell. Might as well plunge right in. "I missed you."

"Yeah?" Tony's face lit up, reminding Flip of a Renaissance painting.

"I kept wanting to see you, but I was struggling with some things. I'm... it's kind of a weird situation."

Tony stepped closer and spoke quietly. "What brought you here?"

"If I were a religious man, I'd call it a revelation."

"A message from God?"

Flip snorted. "I'm not sure he and I are on speaking terms. This was more like the lifting of a veil. I saw with clarity the way things are and what path I should follow. And, uh, that path includes you." He added hastily, "If you want it to."

Tony, chewing on his lower lip, gave Flip such a long look that Flip started to squirm. "I think I do," Tony finally said, making Flip sag with relief. "I mean, Aunt Amelie's machinations aside, I *like* you. I like spending time with you."

Nobody had ever said that to Flip before. Maybe it had been implied in some people's actions, yet in the back of his head, Flip had always suspected that his companions were settling, that he was simply good enough until someone better came along. Now he had to blink back tears. "I have a plan. Do you want to hear about it?"

"You've cranked up my curiosity all the way, that's

for sure. But, shit, I have a meeting in an hour with a potential donor, and then I need to have a discussion with an architect about some work in the former slave quarters." Tony sighed. "Waiting is going to kill me, but *can* it wait? Until after five?"

"Of course." Waiting might kill Flip too, but this wasn't truly an emergency, and besides, it might be better to do this in the evening. Nights were ghostlier than daytimes in New Orleans. And he'd do well to remember that not everyone could be as flexible with their time as he could; Tony had a more traditional work schedule that Flip needed to respect.

Tony gently brushed a thumb over Flip's cheek, the movement less hesitant than Flip would have expected. "Can I say something? You're a good-looking man, but today you're especially handsome. You look like someone who's had a heavy burden lifted."

Flip, who knew he was mediocre at best, smiled. "That's it exactly. I let my burdens go. It feels great."

"I'll look forward to hearing the details."

LEFT with an entire day to fill, Flip wandered. He visited the Jazz Museum, which didn't have anything about Scratch but did help him better understand the history of the genre. He bought a couple of CDs in the gift shop even though he didn't have a player. He'd deal with that another time. Then he went to a history museum on Royal

Street, bought and ate a praline—because why not—and sat for a time on the ghost's bench in Jackson Square. The ghost wasn't there, but the people-watching was good.

A few minutes before five found him pacing anxiously in front of the Bergeron-Catanzaro House. It had occurred to him that Tony might have had second thoughts about... everything, so Flip was relieved when Tony burst out the front door and loped toward him. He was so damned adorable in his button-up shirt and pale green sweater-vest that Flip wanted to gobble him right up. He had to remind himself that Tony was not on the menu.

Which reminded him. "Dinner first?"

"Absolutely."

At Tony's suggestion, they went to a nearby Latin American place, which was a good reminder to Flip of how immigration to this city continued, with newcomers adding flavors and sounds to the already dizzying mix. Flip steered the conversation toward Tony's workday. On the face of it, a couple of meetings and some architectural plans might not have been all that exciting, but Tony's enthusiasm made them interesting. It was a pleasure to see someone so in love with his job.

After insisting on paying the bill, Flip asked, "Ready to head to my place?"

"I've been incredibly patient."

"You have."

Miss Amelie had packed up and left. Flip was

thankful, although he suspected she knew what was going on. He could picture her smug grin.

"Nice place," said Tony, looking around the living room.

"I found it online and sort of chose it at random, mostly because it's on St. Philip Street." At the time it had seemed like a slightly whimsical thing to do, or at least an easy way to make a quick decision. He hadn't possessed the patience to wade through many For Rent listings. And the landlord had been willing to do a three-month lease. Now, however, Flip wondered whether it actually had been simple coincidence. Had he lived somewhere else, he wouldn't have met Miss Amelie or Scratch, and things would have taken a very different trajectory.

"My place is sort of cluttery," Tony admitted. "I tend to acquire interesting old things. And lots of books."

"The curse of the historian, I bet. I have a fair number of books too, but they're in storage in California. I came here with nothing except my suitcase."

"Which the airline has lost."

"Actually, they found it. But I gave it away."

Tony's eyes widened. "How come?"

"I needed to make room."

For a moment, Tony seemed puzzled. Then, as Flip had hoped, he realized what Flip meant. "Aunt Amelie. She said...."

"Yeah. Um, that's sort of part of the larger story I

wanted to tell you. And what I'm going to say is sort of a lot. Want to sit down?"

Tony glanced at the couch and then shook his head. "Let's finish our apartment tour first."

"I'm not nearly as good a guide as you are, but sure."

So Tony admired the view from the gallery, and after that the kitchen and hallway took only a moment. That brought them to the bedroom, and Tony halted in his tracks when he saw the bed. "Holy cow. Did that come with the place?"

"Yeah."

"The Bergeron-Catanzaro House originally had one very like it—there's a painting—but it was lost somewhere over the years." He wandered over to peer more closely and stroke the wooden carvings. Which proved unexpectedly erotic, even though Tony probably hadn't intended it that way. Flip had to look away.

When he turned back, Tony was sitting on the edge of the mattress with an impish smile. His feet dangled due to the bed's height, giving him a particularly youthful aspect. "I'm experiencing bed envy. All I have is a plain one from Ikea."

"This one isn't mine, remember. Just a rental."

It was also as good a place as any to divulge Flip's secrets, which might feel more plausible here than on the utilitarian couch in the living room.

"So," Flip began. He felt slightly dizzy. "I'm not sure where to start."

Tony waited, brows raised.

Time to dive in. Flip managed a weak smile.

"So. I've met Scratch Bergeron."

TONY DIDN'T RUN out of the apartment or call 911. Instead he remained very still on the bed, head slightly cocked, eyes wide. "Literally or figuratively met?"

"Literally."

"He's been dead for a century. And I know you're not an immortal vampire because I've seen you go out in the sun."

That wasn't the response that Flip had expected. "Vampire?"

"The subject comes up surprisingly often in this city."

"Ah. The Anne Rice effect. I'm not a vampire. But... you know how Miss Amelie can... sort of see things?"

Tony tipped his head the other way. He slightly reminded Flip of an inquisitive cat. "I seem to remember that you were pretty skeptical about her abilities," Tony said.

"I was in denial. Because the truth is... I can sort of see things too." Flip held his breath as he waited for a scoff of disbelief or a snort of disgust.

But there wasn't either. Just a slight nod. "You have the Clear Eye?"

"Apparently. I didn't know that until I came here. I'd never heard of it, in fact. Miss Amelie told me that it helps me write—which, by the way, I have been doing like crazy lately. Finished the book I'd been stuck on for so long. But that's not all. I can—"

"—see dead people," Tony finished mildly.

"You're acting like that's no big deal."

"It's better than being a vampire." Tony grinned. "Look, I've heard enough stories about this stuff that I'm at least willing to keep an open mind. And you seem pretty grounded in reality, so if you say you can see spirits, well, maybe you can. But you specifically saw Scratch?"

Flip hadn't realized how important it was that Tony believe him—but it turned out to be incredibly important. Relief flooded him so quickly that his knees went weak and he shuffled over to join Tony on the bed.

"I saw Scratch. We talked. We, uh... kissed."

Finally Tony looked startled. "What?"

"Did you know that you look remarkably like him?"

Tony waited a few moments before speaking again. "Tell me the whole thing. From the start."

Flip complied. He wanted to convey not just the facts, but also the emotions: Scratch's sensuality and loneliness, the quiet wonder of interacting with spirits, the conviction that Scratch's story was inextricably entwined with the story of New Orleans. The words came as easily to Flip's mouth as they'd recently come to his fingers, and Tony listened without interruption.

Finally, silence fell. Not heavy as much as contemplative, and Flip didn't disrupt it. He understood that it was a lot to take in, even for someone as open to things as Tony was.

"You haven't seen him since that night we went to dinner?" Tony finally asked.

"No."

"Is that why you wanted me here? To lure him back?"

Shit. This wasn't exactly a love triangle that Flip had accidentally created—it was some other weird shape that geometry had no name for. And it was awkward as hell.

Flip took Tony's hand and held it loosely, not wanting Tony to feel constricted. "I'm not trying to seduce him. Look, he's been hanging around here for a hundred years, mostly all by himself, and I get the sense that he wasn't the type of person who enjoyed solitude. There must be a reason for it, and I don't think he's waited for a century just to jump my bones."

Some of the hurt had faded from Tony's expression. "Then what?"

Flip smiled.

TWELVE

"Do you honestly think this will work?" Tony ran his fingers gently over the plastic keys.

Flip, pacing the bedroom nervously, shrugged. "Seems worth a try."

The little electronic keyboard had been Tony's idea, a sort of extra enticement, like bait on a hook. He and Flip had taken a Lyft to Target, bought the thing, and dragged it back to Flip's apartment. It now sat on the bed beside Tony. If they were unsuccessful, Flip had no idea what he'd do with an electronic keyboard. Donate it to charity? Maybe he'd learn to play it himself.

At least Tony had been willing to go along with his plan. Flip appreciated that.

"I'm going to open my Eye all the way now," he announced.

"You've never seen him while you were awake, though. What if you can't?"

"I've seen other ghosts outside of my dreams."

Tony nodded. "Okay. Go for it." He braced himself on the mattress as if expecting an earthquake or a gale-force wind.

But Flip simply stood straight, took a deep breath, and mentally pried his spectral eyelid as wide as it would go. The bedroom immediately seemed… more three-dimensional, somehow. The colors were brighter, the shadows deeper, and an invisible energy made his skin tingle. More startling, however, was Tony, who emanated waves of soft, soothing colors, and who was tied to Flip with a glowing filament. Although Flip didn't mention the filament to Tony, Flip found its existence reassuring.

"Scratch?" Flip called. "Can you hear me? I'd like to introduce you to your great-great-great nephew. And we have a piano for you to play if you want."

Nothing happened, so Flip called again, and then a third time. Maybe Scratch had had enough of him. Maybe Flip could reach him only in dreams. Maybe—

"That's Anthony Bergeron?" Scratch stood beside the bed in his snazzy three-piece suit, Homburg cocked and eyes squinting as he stared at Tony. He held the umbrella in one hand.

"You can't tell? He looks just like you."

"He ain't as good-looking as me."

"Um, Flip?" said Tony, barely above a whisper. "Is he…."

"Standing right in front of you."

"I can't see him," said Tony, at the exact same time that Scratch said, "He can't see me."

Shit. This was going to be harder than Flip had expected. He frowned, trying to think of the best way to facilitate matters. But before he could think of anything, Scratch huffed and put his free hand to his hip. "Don't be so selfish, boy. Share your Eye."

Flip hadn't been aware that such a thing was possible, and for a moment he had a gruesome image of plucking out one of his eyeballs and handing it over. Then good sense took over and he moved the keyboard so he could sit close to Tony. "Hold my hand."

Looking doubtful, Tony did. The contact crackled like static electricity, which sent a pleasant frisson down Flip's spine and into his groin. He might have gotten distracted by that if Tony hadn't gasped.

"Scratch!" Tony's voice was choked.

Smirking, Scratch struck a pose. "In the flesh. Well, actually not. My flesh is long gone. But in the spirit."

"I... uh... it's nice to meet you. I've heard a lot about you."

"You ain't." Something desolate showed in Scratch's eyes. "Nobody knows nothing about me."

"That's not true. I was named after you!"

"Nah. There's a lot of Anthony Bergerons. Wasn't me." But Scratch nonetheless seemed slightly soothed.

"It was, and some of the old people, they tell stories about you."

"About the fool who got himself killed 'cause he

couldn't keep it in his pants? I bet that keeps 'em laughing over their beers."

"About your talent as a musician. They say you were the best piano player in Storyville. And they talk about how joyful you were—how you seized life with two hands and made everyone around you happy too."

Scratch's shoulders drooped and he stared at the floor. "Didn't seize it hard enough, did I? It got away from me." He glanced at Flip and then lifted his chin. "I saw him first, you know. Before you. You, you're almost as pretty as I was, you could have anyone you want. You got a whole world full of living folks to choose from. But he's all I got."

Flip wasn't sure how he felt about being the consolation prize, but he kept his mouth shut. He didn't want to antagonize either the living man or the dead one.

"I'm not nearly as popular as you imply," Tony said softly. "And Flip isn't yours. He isn't mine either—he's his own man. But Scratch, you know the two of you have no future together. A living person can't be partners with a ghost. It's not fair to either of you."

"Fair," Scratch scoffed. "Fair woulda meant I got treated the same as folks who didn't have ancestors from Africa. Fair woulda meant the government didn't shut down the houses and rob me of my work. Fair woulda meant Octave Hebert had a nice chat with me and his wife instead of shooting me here in my own bed. Ain't nothin' fair about this world." His tone was angry but his eyes glistened with tears. Flip wanted to reach out to comfort him but feared letting go of Tony.

He aimed for comfort via words instead. "You're right. Lots of shitty things happen to people—good people too—for no reason at all. And unfortunately we can't do anything to fix the shitty things that happened to you. But maybe we can help you a little anyway."

"Nobody can help me. I'm nothing but dust sitting in a *caveau* in Saint Roch's cemetery."

"You're more than that. Think on what Tony said. It's so long after you died, yet your family still talks about you. You are—"

"History," Tony interrupted with a smile. "You are a part of what makes the Bergerons who we are today. I study history—it's my life—because I believe that it's important. Every family, every city, is like a building, each generation resting on the bricks of those who came before. You know, we have a cousin who's a pretty well-known R&B musician. Her genre wouldn't even exist if it wasn't for the music you and your contemporaries created."

Scratch brightened for a moment before shaking his head. "Nobody cares about history."

"I do," said Tony firmly. "Others do too, especially if you give them a compelling story. Not just the dry facts and numbers, but the... the living, beating heart of history. The people who made it. And that's where Flip comes in."

Was that a glimmer of hope in Scratch's expression? Maybe. At least he wasn't disappearing.

"We want to share *your* story," said Flip. "Because we think it's worth sharing."

Scratch narrowed his eyes. "How?"

"We'll write a book about you—together. Not some dreary monograph so overloaded with footnotes and citations that it does nothing but languish in a dusty corner of a shelf. But a *story*. A novel. Something people read on airplanes and on work breaks and then stay up too late because they just can't put the damned thing down."

He'd thought about this a lot, actually. Nonfiction wasn't his strength; he didn't like being constrained too heavily by data and facts. He wanted his readers to taste the foods, smell the scents, hear the clop of hooves and the calls of street vendors, feel his characters' hopes and fears. Of course he'd ground everything firmly in reality, which is where Tony could be invaluable. And with a novel, they'd never have to explain to anyone that their primary source was a ghost. Did the *Chicago Manual* even specify how to cite phantasms?

Frowning, Scratch walked slowly to the window and gazed into the darkness. From the back, Flip would have easily mistaken him for Tony. They had the same stalwart stance, the same broad shoulders that seemed ready for life's burdens.

"Ain't nobody gonna care," Scratch said.

"Tony and the rest of the Bergerons, they care because

you're one of them. But I'm not. I'm a complete outsider, but as soon as I met you, as soon as I learned just a little about you, I wanted more. I wanted to know you because you're worth knowing. Give us a chance and we'll introduce you to the world. They'll want to know you too."

Tony squeezed Flip's hand. It was clear from his tense posture and gnawed-upon lip that Tony was as desperate for Scratch to agree as Flip was.

Before beginning a writing project, Flip would hear the characters whispering faintly in his head. It could be a bit maddening, actually, and writing was his way of making those voices clearer. Now, however, he was experiencing far more than murmurs. His inspiration stood in the same room as him, three-dimensional despite being dead, and Flip's fingers twitched with eagerness to start typing.

"What story will you tell about me?" Scratch asked. "The tomcatting nitwit who was too broke to pay his rent on time, who fucked everyone but never held a lover's interest long enough to settle down?"

"We'll tell the story of a man with human foibles, who was shaped and sometimes constrained by the city and by the times. A devilishly handsome man who dressed sharply and loved music, who didn't seek to harm anyone but wanted to live his life to the fullest. A man who made a lasting impression on others even though he died far too young."

Slowly Scratch turned to face them. "There are plenty of other ghosts in this city. Most of 'em were richer than me. Lots of 'em were more famous. Some of 'em—"

"None of them are you," said Tony firmly. "We're not simply searching for a dead man's story—we want to tell *yours*."

Scratch's expression softened, the guardedness replaced with wonder that emphasized the youth of his mortal years. "You ain't lyin'."

"No."

Scratch leaned the umbrella against the wall and walked toward them. A battered wooden chair appeared and he sat in it, his posture regal. "I'm gonna start by tellin' you about my mama and papa."

"My great-great-great-great grandparents," said Tony, smiling.

"The very same." But then Scratch tilted his head and pointed. "What's that thing there?"

Flip answered. "An electric keyboard. I know you can conjure a real piano, but we thought you might enjoy playing with this one."

And at that, Scratch's eyes sparkled as brightly as if he were alive.

THIRTEEN

"I should probably get that," said Flip as the pounding on the apartment door grew louder. Scratch, who was in the middle of playing something long and bluesy, ignored him, but Tony nodded, set aside his pen, and flexed his writing hand. Flip flexed his too as he walked through the hallway and living room. He'd tried recording Scratch on his phone, but apparently that didn't work with ghosts, so he and Tony had been taking notes for hours. Scratch, on the other hand, seemed indefatigable, spinning endless tales while pounding happily away at the keyboard.

Flip, yawning as he opened the door, found a frazzle-haired young woman in a bathrobe frowning at him from the hall. "It's *late*," she said.

"Oh, shit. Are you 1C?"

She nodded. "Some of us have to work in the morning."

"I am *so* sorry. We lost track of time. I'll ask him to stop."

"Thanks." She thawed a little. "He's real good. We were enjoying the music just fine until it got late. Does he play at a club around here?"

Flip smiled, hoping that Scratch could overhear this conversation. "He used to, but not anymore. His name's Scratch Bergeron."

"I'll look for him on the streaming services. When it's not one a.m.," she added pointedly.

Good luck with that, Flip thought. "We'll keep it down. I am really sorry." He made a mental note to drop off a peace offering as soon as possible. Maybe a bottle of decent wine.

After bidding her good night, he shambled back into the bedroom. Tony gave him a sleepy grin. "Without you touching me, I can hear his music but not his voice. And I can't see him."

"The neighbors can hear him too." Flip sat heavily on the bed, one thigh just barely against Tony's, and addressed Scratch. "I think we'd better shut it down for the night. Neighbors."

"It's never too late for good music, boy."

"It is for people stuck in the nine-to-five. Like Tony, actually." He gave Tony an apologetic look; he'd forgotten it was a weekday.

Scratch rolled his eyes but stopped playing. "I got a lot more stories."

"Good," responded Tony. "We want to hear them.

And after I go over my notes I'll have a thousand questions."

"You'll be back, then?"

Flip was as relieved as Scratch when Tony nodded enthusiastically and said, "I'm going to be counting the minutes."

"All right." Scratch stood, fetched his Homburg from where he'd set it on the bed, and resettled it onto his head. But instead of disappearing right away, he stood there in front of them, looking slightly ragged around the edges, like an old photo.

"I been around a long time," he said. "I'm getting kinda tired. I'm just about ready to rest." They all knew he didn't mean sleep in the regular sense. Tony made a tiny distressed noise and Flip's gut clenched, but before either of them could say anything, Scratch raised a hand. "Don't worry. I'll finish what we've started here. But when I *have* finished, I think I'll be ready for that rest. And that's a good thing. Guess I have you two to thank for it. You'll make sure to tell folks about me, though, right?"

"We'll tell the whole world," promised Flip.

Scratch's answering smile came slowly but spread wide, making his eyes crinkle at the corners. It didn't take a Clear Eye for Flip to know that he and Tony would always remember him like this: youthful, devastatingly handsome, a little cocky, fingers twitching as if a new song was yearning to emerge.

"You're a good man, Flip Devin. Good enough for my favorite nephew, even. So you both listen to old

Uncle Scratch, okay? Take advantage of being young and alive, 'cause that's something you ain't never gettin' back once it's gone." He made a lewd gesture to demonstrate exactly what he meant, winked, and vanished.

Flip and Tony stared silently at each other for a long time. How did you follow an exit like that?

Finally, Tony shook himself. "That was.... I don't have words."

"You're not going to wake up in the morning and decide this was all some sort of weird hallucination? Like maybe I slipped something into your drink at dinner?"

Tony clutched both of Flip's hands. "This is real life, Mr. Devin."

Flip felt... full. Not with food, but with emotions, and they were good ones. He'd jettisoned so many things in order to get here, and the effort had been well worth it. None of those discarded things were worth much, and the vacated space was now taken up with everything he'd once feared to hope for. Optimism. Promise for the future. The possibility of a true home. The beginnings of love, along with all the accoutrements of family and belonging and mutual understanding. The things a soul needed in order to be fully furnished.

When Tony leaned forward to kiss him, that was better still.

And wow, but wasn't that exactly what it meant to be *alive*? To enjoy the pleasures of the moment yet also anticipate that the next moment might be better still?

Flip kissed him back.

It was late and they were both exhausted, but they didn't hurry as they undressed each other. Some things were too good to rush, and every new inch of skin was a revelation to be explored with fingers and mouth. Tony had doused the room lights, but illumination from the street—yellow and green and red—filtered in through the windows, giving the bedroom and the lovers a carnival glow. Although Scratch was gone, Flip imagined he heard the faintest echoes of his music, the jazz piano chords augmented by the drums of beating hearts and the saxophones of lungs.

This was a dream. A delirium. Tony's hands on Flip's shoulders, on his ass, Tony's nipples taut salty treats under Flip's soothing tongue.

Tony was full of delightful surprises. He moaned and gasped freely, every sound making Flip's cock throb, and he didn't hesitate to direct Flip to his favorite erogenous zones or to experimentally discover Flip's. Although his skin was soft, his muscles were more defined than his museum-director clothing had revealed.

"You work out," said Flip in between licks of abdominal ridges.

"I'm a nerd who exercises."

"I don't—"

"You're perfect, Flip. Exactly as you are."

That was the end of discussion, although soft pleas

continued, along with inchoate words of appreciation whispered like a poem. Naked, erect, his curls springing free, Tony could have been an ancient Greek statue come alive, and his smiles proved as wicked as any Scratch could manage, his fingers as nimble on Flip's body as Scratch's were on a piano.

Flip sprawled on his back over the continent-bed, Tony on top of him. Sweet sweat stuck them together. Tony wrapped his long fingers—a pianist's fingers—around both their shafts while Flip, perhaps a vampire after all, sucked at the juncture of neck and shoulder.

And the glowing filament that bound them together wrapped around and around them, connecting but not constricting, an ethereal ribbon of warmth and comfort and power.

Flip fell apart with a howl that surprised him and probably woke up Apartment 1C. He was going to have to add some nice pastries to the peace offering. When Tony came just a few moments later, Flip laughed with pure pleasure and joy.

Nestled against each other, allowing their breathing to even and the ceiling fan to cool them, they chuckled as if sharing a wonderful joke. Nothing in the world had ever felt more right than Tony Bergeron in bed with Flip.

"Stay the night?" Flip asked.

"What's left of it. Don't think I can move anyway." Despite his disclaimer, Tony squirmed around and propped himself on an elbow so he could gaze down at Flip. "You sure know how to show a guy a good time."

"Yeah?"

"Dinner, ghosts, family reunion, history research, music, exceptional lovemaking, cuddling.... What more could anyone want?" He bent to kiss the tip of Flip's nose before collapsing back into his arms.

Flip rolled against him, burying his just-kissed nose into Tony's hair. What more indeed.

FOURTEEN

They overslept. Tony had to call in sick to work, and then they decided that since they were still in bed, they ought to take advantage of that. Their morning sex was as good as the previous night's. Afterward they spent a long time simply lolling in bed as if they were stranded on a desert island, touching each other and talking easily about their plans for telling Scratch's story.

Although Flip would have been content to never return to reality, eventually their hungry stomachs won out. They took turns showering, with Tony borrowing a toothbrush and comb as well as a T-shirt and underwear. "Good thing I have enough to spare," Flip pointed out.

They wandered through the Quarter before settling on a spot for brunch. Flip hadn't been to this place before and liked it immediately, with its slightly wonky brick walls, its scents of cinnamon and frying eggs, and its tattooed, pierced, and dyed-hair waitstaff. Tony and Flip stole bites off each other's plates, laughed at in-jokes, and were generally so cute and lovey-dovey that everyone else in the restaurant probably hated them.

"So," Tony said, not as nonchalantly as he likely intended. "What are you going to do if this project takes us longer than two and a half months?"

"Oh, no way we're going to finish in that timeframe."

Tony speared one of Flip's boudin balls with a fork, transferred it to his own plate, and then said "boudin balls," and giggled like a twelve-year-old. "But you're planning to leave the city then."

"Was planning. But I could stick around. If you don't mind."

There was that sweet smile. "I don't mind."

In truth, Flip's finances would be a little tricky. But maybe he could finagle an extra advance from his publisher, and if not, he could find a day job. He'd had them before. "Then I guess I'll stay." He scooped up and ate a spoonful of grits.

Tony spent a moment thoughtfully squinting at him before apparently reaching a decision. "This is going to sound crazy. But you're a ghost-talking psychic, so bear with me. I know we've barely just met, but... move in with me. My bed's not as epic as yours, but it's big enough for two."

"Seriously?"

"Seriously. I mean, my mortgage is the same whether you're there or not. I've got a bedroom set up as an office, and you'd have it to yourself all day while I'm at work. My neighborhood's quieter than the Quarter but it's still close by. My house has a nice little courtyard, and—" He broke off, snorted, and shook his head. "I sound like a stalker or a real estate agent. The truth is, Flip, I like being near you. A lot. And if you're like-minded, we can make this work."

Flip's first instinct was to say *God, yes!* but he thought it over first. He'd need to keep the St. Philip place until his lease ran out. And then there was the question of what he'd do with himself once this book was finished. Except, he realized, New Orleans was teeming with ghosts, and every one of them was a potential novel. Maybe some of them would be as eager as Scratch to share their stories with the world.

But there was also the fact that he'd never had a lasting relationship with anyone. He pushed them away or scared them off. Maybe, however, that was because none of them were truly right for him. Tony... Tony felt right.

Then he remembered that he'd jettisoned his pessimism and self-doubt along with his luggage, and he grasped Tony's hands across the table. "God, yes," Flip said.

THEY STOPPED off first to buy wine and cake for Apartment 1C and then at a pharmacy for rubbers and lube—both of them giggling like teenagers—and then made their way back toward St. Philip Street. Fluffy clouds sailed through a cornflower sky, trees bloomed, and shopkeepers greeted them from open doorways. In front of Jackson Square, the mule-carts were lined up awaiting tourists, the entire scene a postcard come to life, and the scent of beignets wafted on the light breeze.

Miss Amelie sat at her little table in her usual spot, grinning as they turned the corner. "Well, don't you two look like the cat that got into the cream!" She cackled and clapped enthusiastically.

Holding hands, they stopped in front of her. "I suppose you want us to tell you that you were right all along," said Tony.

"Of course I was, and of course I do. You boys, beatin' your heads against a wall when there ain't no reason for it. Fight against the nasty stuff, but sit back and enjoy the good. And you got plenty of good comin' your way." She nodded for emphasis.

Flip was glad he'd discarded his skepticism. "Thank you, Miss Amelie."

"Well, I don't create the facts, but I sure am happy when I can pass good ones along." She picked up her cards and began shuffling but kept her gaze trained on Flip and Tony. "Now, you know you can't move into Tony's until you're done talkin' to Scratch. Tony's place is out of poor Scratch's range."

"Oh. I hadn't thought about that."

She flapped a hand dismissively. "Not a big thing. Until then, Tony can stay with you."

If Tony minded her decreeing his housing conditions, he didn't show it. "Sure, that'd be fine," was all he said. "It's a nice apartment."

Flip put an arm around Tony's middle and gave a gentle squeeze. "Nicer with you in it."

"Anyhow," said Miss Amelie, "with all the money you're gonna make from royalties, maybe the two of you'll find a bigger house. You could buy yourself one of those la-di-da mansions in the Garden District. Get yourselves a big enough dining room to invite the whole family over for Sunday dinner." She laughed, coughed, and laughed some more.

Tony glanced at Flip. "Neither of us knows how to cook that well."

"Well, boy, your mama and papa will show you when you ask. Maybe your papa will even share that gumbo recipe he's been guardin' so selfishly."

Flip didn't know whether he was having a genuine vision or if it was simply his fertile imagination, but he could picture it clearly. A dozen people crowded around a table laden with food, everyone talking and teasing and laughing at once. Some of Scratch's favorite tunes playing gently in the background. Kids and a dog or two running around, Tony sharing a new bit of family lore he'd dug up, Flip taking it all in while, in the back of his head, plotting his newest book. And there was a ghost as well, an older woman in a long dress who smiled and watched from the shadows, remembering happy times she'd spent in that room when she was alive.

But Miss Amelie was still casting instructions. "Now Flip, you make sure and tell Scratch to stop and say good-bye before he moves on, you hear?"

"Of course."

"And when you are ready to move in with Tony, you boys round up a half-dozen strong young people and someone with a truck."

"I don't have that much stuff," Flip protested. "I could probably fit it all in a grocery bag."

"You ain't fittin' that bed in no grocery bag, now, are you?" She crossed her arms.

"That bed doesn't belong to me."

"Could be a weddin' gift to you both," she replied, confusing Flip.

But Tony burst into laughter. "Aunt Amelie, who owns Flip's apartment?"

Now she was the one looking like a cat who'd gotten into the cream.

Oh. Of course. Well, like she said—he might as well sit back and enjoy the good. "Thank you," he repeated, as Tony bent and kissed her creased cheek.

Then she made a shooing motion. "You get along now. You're keepin' all my clients away when you ought to be taking advantage of what you bought at the pharmacy. Git."

Flip blushed, as did Tony—and Tony looked delicious with that flush on his cheeks. They linked arms and dashed across the street, pausing to wave to Miss Amelie before they entered the building.

This, Flip realized, is how a new life began. New Orleans. His Eye wide open. Boundless creativity. A sense of trust. And, finally, unbelievably, the man of his dreams.

ACKNOWLEDGMENTS

The genesis of this book was a writers' retreat in New Orleans. I'm so thankful to Ari McKay and TL Travis for coordinating this retreat and inviting me, and to all the attending authors for a wonderful experience!

I'm also grateful to Yvonne Farmer and Rochelle Merrill for reading over my draft and ensuring I didn't make any egregious errors. It means so much to me when folks expend time and effort to help me out this way.

Special thanks to my editor, Karen Witzke, who helps my prose shine, and to my proofreader, Allison Behrens. In this case, Allison not only caught my dumb mistakes, but kept me company during the retreat. It was her idea to do a tour of the Beauregard-Keyes House, which of course helped me envision the Bergeron-Catanzaro House.

And finally, "thanks" to several airlines that have sent my luggage on extra adventures. Sometimes inspiration arrives in unexpected ways!

ABOUT THE AUTHOR

Kim Fielding is very pleased every time someone calls her eclectic. Winner of the BookLife Prize for Fiction, a Lambda Award finalist and a Foreword INDIE finalist, she has migrated back and forth across the western two-thirds of the United States and, after a long exile, has recently returned to Portland, Oregon. She's a university professor who dreams of being able to travel and write full time. She also dreams of having two daughters who fully appreciate her, a husband who isn't obsessed with football, and a house that cleans itself. Some dreams are more easily obtained than others.

Kim can be found on her blog: http://kfieldingwrites.com/

Facebook: https://www.facebook.com/KFieldingWrites

and Twitter: @KFieldingWrites

Her e-mail is kim@kfieldingwrites.com

ALSO BY KIM FIELDING

Series

The Bureau

Greynox to the Sea

Love Can't

Ennek

Bones

Stars from Peril

Novels

Rook's Time

Crow's Fate

The Taste of Desert Green

Potential Energy

The Muffin Man

Teddy Spenser Isn't Looking for Love

Hallelujah (with F.E. Feeley Jr.)

Blyd and Pearce

A Full Plate

The Little Library

Ante Up

Running Blind (with Venona Keyes)

Staged

Rattlesnake

Astounding!

Motel. Pool.

The Tin Box

Venetian Masks

Brute

Novellas

Shelf Made Man (December 2024)

Man of His Dreams

Bread Crumbs

Regifted

Bite Me: An Elucidation in Three Acts

Farkas

Ash Believes the Impossible

A Very Genre Christmas

Gravemound

The Solstice Kings

Dei Ex Machina

The Golem of Mala Lubovnya

Refugees

The Dance

Transformation

Summerfield's Angel

The Tale of August Hayling

Phoenix

Grown-Up

The Pillar

The Border

Housekeeping

Night Shift

Speechless

Guarded

The Downs

Short Stories and Collections

Dog Days of December

Firestones

Dreidels and Do-Overs

Get Lit

Christmas Present

Act One and Other Stories

Exit through the Gift Shop

Dear Ruth

Grateful

The Sacrifice and Other Stories

Saint Martin's Day

The Festivus Miracle

Joys R Us